Praise for INFIELES

These stories range from the humid heartland of the Cordilleras to the icy depths of America and the shadowlands of Martial Law and the Drug War. Their concerns are varied as well, peopled by a gallery of characters from an alienated Overseas Filipino Worker to a cuckolded boyfriend, to a Jesuit Volunteer and mute witness to extra-judicial killings.

Quintin Jose Pastrana is especially good when drawing characters who are wry, complex, and postcolonial, interacting as they do beyond dialogue and into our culture of dreams, nostalgia, and subterfuge. These stories have heart, as his own heart is in our country, not in Oxford and Cambridge. His inventiveness and fidelity turn Philippine history on its head, giving it a different angle, and thereby showing us how we arrived at this mess after all—because we have allowed the Others to all but erase our true stories and personal histories. —**Danton Remoto**, author of *Riverrun, A Novel* and Gawad Balagtas achievement awardee, Writers' Union of the Philippines

———•••———

An idealistic young campaigner, a surgeon, a cello, a girl following her destiny, the best man, a little girl's guardian— behind them, around them, the Church and the nation, drug smugglers, politics and community loom ominous, tentacles reaching into the lives of Filipino everymen and women. Quintin Pastrana's vision of the people and the country, in the country and out of it, delves deep, brings up promise, disillusionment, resignation, and immanent hope. Vivid and dark, he conjures up places distant yet familiar; this is exciting, complex, thought-provoking. —**Amal Chatterjee**, author of *Across the Lakes* and senior tutor, University of Oxford

Praise for INFIELES

Loneliness, grief, isolation, and struggle all search for a voice in Quintin Pastrana's distinctly Filipino exploration of dispos-session. We are given glimpses into unquiet souls dispossessed of their identity, their passions, and their home. Ultimately, these pilgrims—as the author himself has described them—find their place in language, as Pastrana guilelessly takes from the dark and distressed, the weary and woeful, to find the 'colours within.' —**Marga Ortigas**, journalist and author, *The House on Calle Sombra*

———•◖◗•———

Quintin Pastrana writes about isolation. About lonely people searching for a reason for being, immigrant journeys through desolate roads in adopted lands, road trips through the hin-terlands of his archipelago. He writes about the desperate twists and turns of bodies and souls.

The stories resonate, and the reader—Filipino or not—will find his or her own story woven among the delicate phrases, perhaps as the commuter on the way to work, "fermenting with caffeine and the dregs of last night's antics." Or perhaps as the uncle annoyed by the youth "brandishing their selfie sticks like brooms" everywhere he goes.

Quintin knows well why "the best way from a speakers' lips to an audience's heart is through stories. It's in our DNA, from the street gossip we hear to the ghost and fairy tales we grew up with," "across meridians, and into an archipelago where the myths and memories matter." His vivid descriptions flesh out tales of our lives, are sometimes playful, sometimes dark, but always from the particular point of view of the Filipino who dreams of home, whoever and wherever that may be. —**Yvette Fernandez**, author and editorial director, Summit Media

Quintin Pastrana works "infidel"—the title's *Infieles*—like a violin's cat gut bow, along strings that can screech if touched less than nimbly. But the infidel in his hands sounds the human as Filipino: haunted, spellbound, tormented, mock courageous, desirous, spent. Pastrana knows their various patois and codes. He also knows their overlords, about whom his language is barbed. *Infieles* is a Philippines that he wishes he can protect, even in fiction, but can't. He can only be vulnerable like the rest, avoid screeching, and find the precise timbre to convey the infidel's precariousness. —**Marian Pastor Roces**, independent curator and critic

Published in the United States
Centiramo Publishing, New York, NY
www.centiramopublishing.com | info@centiramopublishing.com

Art consultant: Janet Frances White
Book layout: Pierce Centina
Cover image titled "All Too Well" © 2023 Poula Sitjar
Used by permission through the courtesy of Ysobel Art Gallery
Profile and back cover photo of the author by Raena E. Abella

ISBN-13: 978-1-958406106
ISBN-10: 1-958406-10-4

Library of Congress Control Number: 2023938627

FIRST EDITION
4 6 8 10 12 14 16 18 20 19 | 17 15 13 11 9 7 5 3
Designed and printed in the United States of America

INFIELES
TWELVE FILIPINO STORIES

QUINTIN JOSE V. PASTRANA

GentiRamo
Publishing

Pas besoin de gril: l'enfer, c'est les autres.
Jean-Paul Sartre, *Huis-clos*

TABLE OF CONTENTS

Table of Contents

Introduction

Filipinos have had the most bizarre experiences engaging the Other: from colonisers old and new, to fellow migrants and rivals up the crab pot and food chain, to our native, gaudy, and inner selves. Maybe not as 'hellish' as Sartre depicts, or as adversarial as the title implies. But like a dull wound from a rusty *balisong*, the impact is haunting, the effects lasting, and you are never the same after the moment a cut proves blood.

This book tries to forage and curate the flayed pieces of a culture still in search of itself. These twelve stories and the generation of lives that inhabit them—these lost pilgrims, from the hinterlands to overseas—have come together as strange bedfellows to a crowded party of an unknown host. They are fragments to a mosaic that I hope will be recognizable to, if not resonate with my own people and those outside our barely porous circle—who are just beginning to know us, even as we struggle to embrace ourselves.

It is important to note that this work is a piece of fiction (hopefully a decent one), and any similarities to real-life characters, settings, or actions are purely products of the reader's imagination. All flaws and artistic shortcomings are entirely my own.

I wish to thank Dr. Clare Morgan, Jane Draycott, Marti Leimbach, Jenny Lewis, and the wonderful tutors at Oxford for giving me a chance and letting me find my voice in verse and prose. Special thanks go to Amal Chatterjee, for your unrelenting wisdom and patience in helping me forge this collection into as decent a shape as it can ever be. And to Jing Hidalgo and Danton Remoto, for helping these stories come full circle, to come home with the gravitas of identity. To my schoolmates, friends, mentors, publisher, and Muse, thank you for weaving inspiration and life into this work. To

my dear family and friends, for your patience and tough love—
you are the most nurturing critics in the world. Constanza
Daniela Gonzalez, Regie Plana-Alcuaz and Anya Plana-Hutt,
Inez Togle-Vasquez, and Manang Nellie Ballola, for bridging
my cultural and linguistic ignorance in the stories of your
communities, and almost forgiving how I rendered them. Lastly,
to Lolo Papa, Ambassador Vicente L. Pastrana: thank you for
tracing ever so faintly a path I could find and call my own.

February 1995

Campaign Stop

IN THE DARKNESS I FISHED out an old, white sock from the drawer.

My tubes are usually tied in knots, taut enough to stay together, comfy enough to loosen for a quick getaway.

This was a straggler. With a hole in it. It was 4:12 a.m. and I held onto it in a state of restless stupor. In a few minutes, the phantom alarm would ring in my head again like clockwork.

My condition and temperament leaves me little else but a distaste of the unfamiliar. Less margin for error, more time to figure out the critical things, and certainly not to wade into something as trivial. Like the past.

I am up again, staring at an open knapsack and my arsenal: tampons, stapler guns, Kitkats and Mentos for me, and Ricola for my boss. The sock has found its match, and they snugly hold on to my ankles. I zip the bag, walk out of my parents' house, and into my new silver blue car. My feet test the brakes, step on the clutch, and then the gas as the Honda goes into reverse. My heels dig in and neither feels a hole where it should be.

I've got a rally to advance, and there's hell to pay if FMR gets there ahead of me. I needed to get out of here.

The haze filtered the dusk light into a stifling grey, and as soon as I got off the last traffic light, I felt free. The kitsch of billboards, their ads of whitening cream on ageing celebrities and political figures, and the mottled concrete I drove under gave way to an open sky and quickening road. I was barely ahead of schedule. Forgetting my caffeine drip, my thoughts wandered as I fought to stay awake.

The pager buzzes. My heart skips a beat. Just Martin sending his love. Telling me his fellow residents are giving him the night off. *Dont b L8 hon drive safe & stay kool. Celebr8 l8r.* Messages like these, and what we had, put me at ease. We shared just as many years as what separated us in age, and it almost helped me to trust myself, against my deeper impulses, like this leap into FMR's world.

Then came another: this time the stubbles on my legs start stiffening. "ETA 1300." I had a couple of hours left (2.5 to be exact), and Morris's message told me he would be ferrying the Senator at hyper speed and they might just get there ahead of me.

I remember Dad nagging me to break the engine in gently, but I just floored the pedal and yanked the stick into fifth. At over 120 kph, the *caballero* trees appeared to leap out with their orange flame buds, pacifying my angst, hiding within them the black shiny worms that gather on the ground when the flowers die.

As the roar settled, I ease into the memory of my job interview. Six months already and I still keep replaying it in my head. That first time I wandered through the preliminary vetting, the hall of bookcases, and stepped into his study.

FMR TOOK OFF HIS spectacles, and set them down a pile of committee rulings. His eyes were curiously attentive, dark but full of outpouring. One of them kept on twitching, something I'd seen as a harbinger of brilliance or anger forthcoming. I came prepared with my *codigo*, scribbled on my palm—about how I wanted to be a litigator, then an international jurist bringing despots to The Hague, and how in the meantime, I could cut my teeth as a policy wonk, passing the women's rights legislation he wrapped himself in, all while helping him with the youth vote in the May elections. My smile was bold, but I gritted my teeth, ready for interrogation armed with my ambition and OCD. He stood up, his paunch barely concealed by the *piña barong* he straightened out as he transferred his gaze from me toward the window, where the sun was just setting.

"Tell me. What's your favourite novel...and why?"

I wanted to be clever and tell him it was like asking what my favourite city was, even if I'd only read mostly about them.

"Gatsby." It just leapt out of me. "Because I want to leave and come back as someone else. Someone with the means to reach my dreams."

"Even if it meant losing sight of it, if it already lay behind you? He interjected. Fitzgerald, Dumas, and even Dr. Rizal—they're more connected than you think. The desire to disappear quietly, beyond memory and return reborn, to face your unwitting foes, and win back love and all its promises. We all feel it. Want it. Even if we fail to recognize who we once were. I once almost did... But we'll save that for another time. You will start tomorrow, and we all have some work to do."

JUST AS I THOUGHT I got away from the city, I entered a newly christened one. The road narrowed as the dust-ridden car crossed the archway into Lipa. Overseas remittances and the unbridled demand for housing had sheared off bucolic farmlands, replacing them with faux European villas and row-houses of poured concrete.

I parked by one of the remaining trees, its orange flowers strewn on the ground; their dark larvae underneath, feeding on the last days of summer.

I unfurled the posters in the strangling heat, then I groped for the stapler gun from my knapsack. I looked around for branches that hadn't already been crucified by the other staffers.

Bernie came up to me as I surveyed the area. He always managed to arrive an hour earlier, with surplus gear and an eye for detail.

"Hay nako, tulungan nga kita," he teased me as he grabbed a sheaf of my posters. He unfolded his ladder, and started pumping industrial grade staples, and my candidate's meme, onto the tree trunks around the plaza.

I removed my shoes and summoned my childhood skills to climb the tallest one. After some contortions, I nailed the last, largest banner in place. Right where FMR would see it when he emerged from his motorcade. I slid down the tree, its bark slowing my descent, white cotton threads from the balls of my feet coming undone as I touched the ground. I marvelled at my handiwork. His once-chiseled face—an earlier, retouched photo—and his name emblazoned underneath the neckline, now looked upon the town, as T.J. Eckleburg once did upon West Egg's valley of ashes.

The town, this province, mirrored the others in Southern Luzon—a congealment of the teeming masses, controlled by political warlords on one hand and the Catholic dioceses on the other. 1995 was the new 1984.

All in all, a gross tally of humanity: 1.2 million hapless voters. Enough of a block to swing us over the top. FMR and I, along with the other senatorial candidates and their ragtag retinue, were at the sweet spot.

I entered the cathedral to escape the sun and the great unwashed that grew around the plaza, and took refuge near the altar under the only working electric fan. From there, amidst the ivory heads of the saints, and the Stations of the Cross carved from disemboweled forests, I watched as people wallowed in the Middle Ages.

Bejewelled matrons with their white-laced *belos* lay prostrate, sweat and rosary beads hanging from their flabby necks. Each waited for her turn to kiss the hairless, almost embalmed fingers of the well-fed Archbishop Arguilla.

I heard shouting by the freshly painted Romanesque entrance. A small, uniformed man was waving his truncheon, trying to evict this *taong grasa* I thought I'd seen on the way in—faceless, half-clothed, his kind multiplying across the landscape. The veiled women shook their heads in disgust and then quickly went back to their glorious mysteries.

I felt like vomiting from all this lunacy until *my* candidate appeared, crossing the pews and shaking hands along the aisle. I remembered to grab my notebook. Just a month before, he scolded me: "Write everything down, *Olivia*! Memory is treacherous..."

I rushed towards him, and cleared my throat.

"There you are.....All set?" he said.

Campaign Stop

"Sir... I have something to tell you."

"Not right now. Ah, there he is." He strode down the aisle.

"*Your Eminence*..." It was his turn to smooch the ring.

"Mr. *Senator*...Good of you to come...our parishioners have high hopes for you..."

"Did you meet my aide..."

"Yes, of course...a fine specimen....What's a virgin like you doing in a job like this?"

"Well, I wanted to serve and..." He waved me off and looked at his benefactor.

"Your support to our diocese's pilgrimage to St. Peter's this year is *most* appreciated. You did receive the letter I sent a *month ago, no?*" The bishop sneered at me.

"I will gladly look at it after the campaign, and see if it still fits our pork barrel. As you know, the poverty programmes come first, *Your Grace*."

"We will be *waiting* for your generous response—*if* you get re-elected, Mr. Senator."

"I will be responding *most decisively*—when I do." He flashed his signature Cheshire cat smile, then turned around. It was my cue to follow and smile myself, and we left just as the lector urged everyone to rise and break into a dirge.

"Medieval Prick," the Senator muttered as we shuffled off the centre aisle, and finally we were outside. "One day, they finally won't matter. Until that happens, you just have to humour them and subtly put them into their proper places... There isn't a Catholic vote, *but I'll be damned if there still isn't a Catholic veto.*"

More people milled around the senator as we walked outside the cathedral and he greeted them warmly and clasped their hands. He clapped their shoulders and hugged the grandmothers as the camera flashes popped in the cloudy afternoon.

When the crowd had cleared, we resumed walking. The senator spoke again. "Tell Bernie he did a great job. We'll need more of the same to catch up with the bitch."

The polls showed him at number 2 amongst the senatorial candidates. With the 12 slots now being contested by has-been comedians, slacker scions, and faded beauty queens, he already stood out and could just coast along. But there was the Presidency, of course, and we would do well to harbour these with a good showing at the senatorial re-election, and more legislative coups ahead. No slacking off now.

The rally started late, as expected, but more than I feared. Martin and I had our 7 p.m. moved back to 9:30 p.m. I was always of the *under-promise, over-deliver* kind, but even this new ETA was cutting it really fine.

Twelve candidates would speak, and at the clip of about 10 minutes per speech, with equal opportunity given to the plodders and the entertainers. The easy way to win was through a song-and-dance repertoire, one of the staffers gloated, and a medley usually did the trick. All told, I would still get out of there in time and speed it back to my resident surgeon boyfriend.

This was only my second rally, and I already knew what I was up for. Everyone was always sitting on a veritable firing line, like a motley crew of entertainers waiting for their cue.

To play fair given the audience's diminishing attention, the coalition organisers put us close to last, with the alibi of going by alphabetical order. So from A to R we went, and what a pathetic medley matinee we had in store. Most of the crowd just lapped it up, along with the packed *merienda* and tetra pack Kool Aid knockoffs to keep them engaged.

First was this coup d'etat plotter, hirsute and macho, his belly straining in the same fatigues he had sported in the 1986 People Power revolution. Despite the paunch and the slurred speech, the men, women and children swooned as he

Campaign Stop

clenched his fists and snarled about killing all the gangs, drug lords, and criminals he himself was coddling on the side.

Next up was the silicone-stuffed wife of a dead general. Even I forgot what she was saying amid the thick heat and her considerable assets barely contained under a sweaty blouse. Then followed the erstwhile Goebbels of the Marcos dictatorship, who resurrected his career through his resurgent loyalist network. Here he was, in his Marian blue, touting his "Pro-God, Pro-Life, Pro-Family" values. Who could argue with that in the land of boiling frogs, motherhood, and amnesia? That's when I went a step further than Fitzgerald: you could hold opposing sensations at once—one of retching, begging for pity for the country, while wanting to burn someone alive— yet still keep smiling at the hapless crowd. My *consuelo de bobo*: just like Judas, he didn't make it to the magic roster when the counting was done and dusted.

A few decent re-electionist candidates, shriveling under the heat, decided to sing together, matching campaign vests and all, this ditty and managed to insert an *"Iboto n'yo kami"* line right into the stanza. Not too clever, but it cut the ebbing time, and the clouds gathered to mollify everyone.

One of the few saving graces of the campaign showed up. One of the *barrio* doctors who made good, pint-sized but big enough to matter. Enough to get on the Party slate and before that rise to Health Minister, taking on the Magisterium with his promise to make family planning available in every village. He was the only one whom I'd forgiven for cracking jokes and catchy slogans, while his army of volunteers spread out guerrilla-style and did the teach-ins as he once did as a young man. Even after a diatribe from the mighty Church, he managed to land 5th.

Then it was her turn. Daughter of a former head of state, whose only memorable achievement was to stand by in adulation when his successor lay down Martial Law on my elder brother's generation. The runt outspent us by 10:1, thanks to the manoeuvres of her frankenhog of a spouse and their litter of accomplices who had the feckless loyalty of bleached sheep and the collective IQ of a pork rind. Here we were, on a shoe-string campaign, right behind her. And with the block votes coming from FMR's overpopulated region coming in, there was a chance we would squeak by and never look back. She came prepared—with a canned speech and a surprise guest. Joining her on stage, in a matching outfit and made-for-TV medley, was her "box-office twin," Nora Moreno. The crowd quaffed it all down, swayed along, not unlike the hysteria I'd seen upon leaving the cathedral.

A couple more snoozers went on about free jobs, free schooling, free everything.

I looked out at the crowd.

No matter what I'd thought about the hapless sheep these folks were, I could spot a few faces in the crowd. Some elderly, in their *barong tagalogs* and Sunday best, representing a time when politics wasn't fully perverted. In a corner, with arms folded—young students, with jeans and tank tops that would've been banned in the church. All of them, looking for something real beyond the pandering slogans, mind-numbing jingles, and gaudy gestures.

Amidst all these, I conjured up the time I would be up there and how I would change the discourse—less histrionics, more meat—without losing the crowd. I'd frame things differently, take the cliché of the family as a "basic unit of society" and our proud "matriarchal culture" and stand it on its head. Talk about maternal health clinics to give family planning choices (*note to self: steer clear of abortion rights*) across the 1,492 municipalities and 43,240 villages that don't have them. Get the World Bank and qualified corporations to bank-roll a rural electrification and microfinance programme run by women, so their husbands don't fritter it away on prostitutes, cockfighting, and pomelo gin. Reverse fiscal allocations from Imperial Manila and allow local governments to build their own agenda that fit their needs, and channel them into empowerment programs with annual audits, not white elephants and lined pockets. It would be my agenda, taking a giant leap from my boss, and I wouldn't even need pork barrel like FMR and all his contemporaries.

I snapped out of my daydream as the rains set in. It was his turn. The crowds were about to scatter, but then he walked off the stage. In an instant, he stood among the audience, and they cleared a few feet around him to let him speak. I strained the other way amidst a sea of rainfall and body odour just to keep the eye contact that close-ins needed to keep with their principals all throughout.

"If you want to know what I'll really do, the kind of laws you need, what I'll do for you if you re-elect me, you can ask Olivia, my staffer. She's the expert and I learn from her." He pointed to and smiled at me, already shivering from the downpour. Somewhere in that gathering of pressed flesh I could hear Bernie snickering, "Yes, that's right, it's the young who will show the way." He then switched into the vernacular, and my mind, with my barely decent Tagalog fluency, fought to keep up and translate it in my blue-blooded head:

"This campaign is increasingly about money. My opponents and colleagues have poured everything in just to get elected, and when they do, think about how they and I will try to get that money back. But I'm here to tell you something more important.

"...We have always said money is important. It is good to have money. But the more important thing is strong human values and strong human efforts to excel. You may have all the money in the world, but it will be lost unless you have good human values and you strive to excel. That must come from within. It cannot come from America. It cannot come from the government. It cannot come from anybody. It must come from you, the Filipino.

"And for you to remember that, I will share with you a story. Remember Cesar Legaspi? He was our National Artist. When I was practicing law, I made his will and kept it in the vault. He went abroad for six months. When he came back, he gave me a one-meter long painting. His paintings, [even] one foot long, are worth over half a million pesos. So that is my trophy painting. If you come to my house, I'll show it to you. The painting is in all different shades of green.

"When he gave it to me, I asked him, '*Ka* Cesar, how were you able to paint this when you are colour blind?' Because Cesar Legaspi, our master of colours, was indeed colour-blind. He could not distinguish green from red. So, I asked him, 'How do you paint the various shades of green?' And he said, 'The colour green outside, that is important, but you must find the colours within you. Then the paintings are beautiful.'

"We too, must find the colours within us. That is what we as a people are longing for. We keep getting bad news and bad advice and bad opinions all over. We must find the colours within us. If we are able to motivate our people to find the colours within them, we shall finally achieve development in our country.

"It is not money; it is the heart, it is ideas, it is our beliefs, it is our legends, it is our courage that will make us grow. And that is my only message. Development cannot be done by money alone. Development cannot be done by materials alone. It must begin with the spirit. It must begin with the heart. It must begin from within us, within the talent, ingenuity and creativity of the Filipino. Then we can have true development in real time. *Maraming salamat po.* I hope you remember."

The crowd's applause was expected, but not raucous like what came after the song-and-dance gigs of his colleagues, or the mindless clapping that followed them. It felt like it crested on the rainfall, gentle and contagious. Then, with a couple more speakers left, the people finally began to leave.

I almost pitied the last two candidates. With the continued downpour and no more packed food, they faced an almost-empty and wet basketball court strewn with *styro* food containers and the smell of urine. The other candidates had already executed their French exits as soon as they'd finished, off to their gaudy, debauched weekends before the circus came to another town.

Except for a handful of stragglers, who I thought were looking for another meal, it was all over. I thought of a corollary of Stalin's dictum, and felt that as the mass of the great unwashed disappeared, the ones who stayed had regained their humanity. A woman, possibly in her early thirties—how poverty disguises age so well—approached us. She brought along her six children, all gaunt with big bellies, all clinging on to her as she held on to the tiniest one, slung on a dirty blanket. They all shivered from the steady rain. FMR winked at me; I knew the drill: I unleashed my notebook, ready to take their details (names, village addresses, requests which we would deliver in a fortnight). She went past my *cordon sanitaire*, and went straight to the Senator.

"*Naniniwala po kami sa inyo, Senador.*"

"*Salamat, hija. Ano po ang maipaglilingkod namin sa inyo?*" the Senator asked.

"*Malala na po ang kalagayan namin. Gusto ko po lamang na ipapangako ninyo na patuloy ang laban ninyo para sa mga kagaya namin.*" And with that simple wish—not to be forgotten through his work—they brought us both to an unaccustomed silence. Before he and I could even counter, she had already left, the children looking back at us, as their shadows faded past the lamppost. Thunder dragged back into nightfall. I realized I'd left the pager in the car, and when I got there, I saw Martin's frantic messages beeping madly. It was half-past seven, barely enough time, but better late than never. I called out to Morris, begged him to use the massive Motorola no staffer was allowed to even come near. In hindsight, with all that radiation from those clunkers, it was a good policy.

I bent to reach for it inside the passenger door, called the pager operator, hesitated, then dictated: *Pls go ahd & eat, so sori hon, wl make it up to you...it's still my bday 'til mdnyt and VDay dis wkd;).* My pathetic attempt at intimacy, with a slightly older but even more wooden man. I knew after messing up the last few times, it was going to take a lot of penance with Martin, who bent over backward despite the tyranny of his residency, and always knew how to collect. I thought I heard a chuckle from the faceless agent at the other end of the line as I jammed my finger on the large red button.

As I wiggled out of the car, there he was standing right behind, looking at me with pursed lips.

"I hear it's someone's birthday...Let's celebrate."

"Sir, I have a..."

"A date? You do now...and an important one."

"Uhmm..."

"We're also celebrating my daughter's birthday, but knowing her bedtime—and this—I already asked to make this up tomorrow and Valentine's with SAR Saturday...Tell him you'll do the same, and we'll honour them over dinner. Tell me more about him in the car, I'll get Morris to show us to my favourite place."

I figured it pointless to send another excuse through, and noddingly smirked at my Boss. We both squeezed into my car, then Morris drove off in his for us to follow.

I hadn't had time to dry off, and neither of us prepared for the rain. Still, with showers gone and the tricycles piling on the road out, the heat reasserted itself and I had to turn the aircon on for my passenger. I figured we'd have at least half an hour of driving, and it was on the way back, so I might get home eventually, with a good story to tell apart from all the *lambing* I'd need to shower Martin with. I just let go, stayed in the present, and made my thinking visible to my boss.

"So how do you keep this up, stop from getting frustrated with the audience? I mean, the system's so messed up—the audience so—ignora..." Just then he cut me off.

"You never patronize them given what you and I have!" He had a legendary temper, and I knew this was just a smidgen of it.

"But sir, don't you see it? What's the point of all these policies and beautiful words, when most of them don't get it, and these losers keep getting elected because of them?"

"Don't you think that's all the more reason to keep fighting? If no one else, who will?"

I nodded, even if I barely agreed.

"And remember. The best way from a speakers' lips to an audience's heart is through stories. It's in our DNA, from the street gossip we hear to the ghost and fairy tales you and I grew up with. You just have to find a way to get all that good stuff in there, to them, through those stories. Then they will understand, and do better."

"Yes sir, but at the rate we're going, we're 86 million Filipinos now, in a decade over 100. And every year, there'll be poorer, larger, more helpless families to reach out to, bamboozled by these clowns and Pharisees, who'll never even get half the chance I did...and I'm not even content!" I was being carelessly real.

"As opposed to what?" He slammed his fist on the dashboard. "I had the chance to live the life of picket fences and picnics, commuter trains and college funds, just like the rest of my generation who left. But I came back, put all these grand ideas to work, and I never looked back. Not for a moment."

It was dark in the car, but I knew he was looking away, at the vast open fields, thinking if he really meant it, knowing what little left lay ahead of him and the country he knew. His voice changed, from gruff to gentle, as he turned to me again.

"Speaking of stories. Did you ever hear about the one about the little clock?"

"No, I think I missed that one growing up." I frowned.

"Well, dear, that's because it's an early one of mine." He cleared his throat and started out as a story to his daughter. I eased up on the gas, let Morris stretch ahead, and relaxed in his company.

"There once was this little clock, who wanted to get to the end of the day when his master would come back home so she could watch over him, then watch him wake him up again. He looked up to the grandfather clock across the room, because of his age and stature. One day, he couldn't help but ask him how he managed to stay so calm, and so wise in doing his noble work of marking time. The grandfather clock bent over, smiled with his ivory, moustached face, and told him something he'd never forget: 'My dear, you have a lifetime of joys, sorrows, and friends to make and watch over...and the only way that makes it all worthwhile is to go from tick, to tock—being ever-present, moment by moment with grace and attention to make everything count.'"

I could feel him smile and believe again, and just in that moment, I let myself succumb to that mawkish reverie.

Morris took a left, and I followed until we reached a faint sign that read "Rose and Grace." It was 9:30 p.m., and the last of the diners had gone home. I could hear the pager beeping, and then I just fiddled with it and yanked the battery out as FMR opened the door and wandered inside.

The dinner was a big blur, and I don't know if it was the *lambanog* that flowed freely. Or that it was the first time I tried *bulalo*, the house specialty, with its massive shanks of beef and golden marrow.

FMR kept joking that he learned the hard way of never eating the dish in a restaurant located next to a cemetery or hospital, which is why R&G was the chosen place. He taught me how to use a barbeque stick to jab into the bone opening, reaching all the crevices. Then at the right time, overturn the femur onto the plate, and then bluntly tap the base until the marrow gurgled onto the plate, to be mixed with the steaming rice, then wolfed down before it congealed on your throat, and swig the *lambanog* to hit the spot. I'd never experienced anyone with this mirthful abandon for life, from words to sustenance.

We shed our defence mechanisms along with our table manners as we devoured every morsel of boneless *tawilis*, punctuated by occasional slurping of the syrupy gelatin cubes in the *sago't gulaman*.

I thought I saw his gaze stay longer below my neck longer than I thought decent so I folded my arms while he pretended to keep telling stories from his early life. It wasn't the first time, and surprisingly, I didn't feel offended. Someone I have always looked up to suddenly became more human, and it created between us a newfound propinquity.

A few weeks back, Bernie took me aside and warned me that people were already talking. The typical principal-staffer shenanigans. I laughed then, for it was absurd and frankly too early on. But it also felt strange. Empowering even. I felt that connection tinged with pity every time we'd be alone, when he would coax a few details here and there and then offer something of himself—a story, a compliment, an instruction— almost as a present. This happy unease — this poorly-cloaked ardour—was mine alone. I knew if I could bear it, it would make the ascent just as satisfying as when I climbed up that tree and saw everything. How things, then and now—even the sordid—all looked so small and harmless, and worth the deed.

Just then, he asked for the bill and looked at his watch (I didn't even bother anymore with mine). There was a pause in his hoarseness, one you could feel beyond the gust of his voice. One that already betrayed the metastasis that whispered through his bowels. Morris left the table to start the car. FMR's face, once and always handsome, turned and shone on me as if there was only mine to behold in the room. His hands trembled on the table, trying to reach mine. He looked gravely at me and said: "You are young, there is much more to do. The best and the worst challenges are still ahead of you. You might be as stubborn as me, but try to remember when these times come: *Never lose the power to walk away from it all.* I wish I had sometimes. But we are what we do, and I can still live with what's in front of me."

There was more love revealed in those moments than I was to come home to, or have ever since. As if the world had opened up that night, and then sealed shut seven years after. The night I flew out to take on my *Juris Doctor* enveloped the same dusk that flooded FMR's hospice room with the last of his defences breached.

I entered a darkened apartment, still fresh with his scent. Near the untouched dinner cleaved with a surgeon's delicate hands, lay a small, empty velvet box: the last tenderness I would receive from Martin.

The day we were graduated, before the alcohol and weed set in...something was carved into me, something I cannot escape in moments like these. Even now I could still trace the words as it rained on my ears, this Jesuit prayer that stood out from all the benedictions that day.

> *What you are in love with,*
> *what seizes your imagination,*
> *will affect everything.*
> *It will decide what will get you out of bed in the morning,*

What you will do with your evenings,
How you will spend your week-ends,
What you read, what you know breaks your heart,
and what amazes you with joy and gratitude.
Fall in love, stay in love, and it will decide everything.

THE LAW CAUGHT UP with some, as it usually does outside the country we both left behind. I even managed to chalk up a fair share of despot convictions for other hapless states, without any of the horse trading I'd have done if I'd left the international jurisdictions and brought my trade back home.

Coming back to settle my parents' affairs, within the same walls and the cloister of books that lulled me before that journey, I still come back to that day.

I looked at the empty room, traced the hole in the frayed sock for one last time, and placed it back in the drawer.

The Haunted Cello

THE MIRAGE GAVE WAY to a sharp curve and an elbow from Diane. The moon was full, and matched the feeble street lamps that traced the winding hills. After crossing an abandoned track, we entered a narrow road.

"Cormier Alley, this better be it."

It should have been; it was already half past ten. We drove downward at what looked like a clearing; but as we closed in, we found out that it was actually a cliff. We could hear the icy river crackling at what felt like a hundred meters below.

"Make it fast. I don't care about dinner or Darwin anymore—this isn't what I signed up for. Did you see how dodgy this place is?! I just wanna go home."

So did I. As I closed the door behind me, I cursed under my breath at how foolish this all looked: two hapless, freezing, Southeast Asian graduate students, in an abandoned steel town in the middle of a godawful winter night. It was so quiet you could hear a raccoon get an erection.

THE SELLER INSISTED HE would not deliver. "That's why it's priced so low, *brother.*" A mocking e-mail, but what else could I expect from an e-bay vendor. *From Allentown, Pennsylvania of all places!*

It didn't matter. At six hundred twenty bucks (on BUY IT NOW, no less), a 19th-century cello was a steal. Lessons were tucked away at the back of my ten-year plan, but I already called dibs on the instrument. With 186 positive feedback points and 90% rating, the seller looked legit enough. Better than mine, at least, and enough for me to put on my duffel, take the Blue line to Reagan National, and chance a rental.

On the way I called Diane. She was in dissertation Purgatory, and I thought I could give her a hall pass out of it. Just 3 ½ hours to be exact, including a dinner in Philly with Darwin. She hadn't seen him since the summer tryst in Negril. Since he hadn't called, it might be worth her while to 'stop in' with me to try and make him jealous. I couldn't care any less. I wanted the soon-to-be-mine *C. Frederik and Sons* handiwork. And a warm dinner at Cuba Libre in Old Town, on the way back from *Hick-town*, would be welcome. I had it all mapped out, so to speak.

Except that the server was down this morning. At the airport, none of those GPS *thingamajigs* were available. Waze was still a decade away. We would wing it, of course: one of those charming inborn traits of our people. After token resistance, Diane said "yes," and even volunteered to print out the MapQuest trail. I'd pick her up in Georgetown, then off to the Beltway, then up the I-95.

There was another problem. After they swiped my card, I took the papers, got out of the parking lot, and in my struggle to find my keys without my fat gloves, I left my phone somewhere.

It wouldn't appear until much later, after I passed for Diane, shrinking amid the flurries.

"Where were you!? And why didn't you call?" She figured I had lost the phone.

"Again!?"

As we turned into the I-395, it suddenly hit me as we drove alongside the Pentagon. I slammed the brakes. A sheaf of snow rushed forward, and with it, three thuds. And then, a crushing sound on the left. As we stopped to look back, there it was—my poor Nokia. It was splayed across the icy road and disemboweled further by Beltway Bandits rushing back to the burbs. It had been left to freeze-ride on top of the Camry all this time. My life. And my only way of reaching Mr. Grieger.

Amidst Diane's braying, I parked the car on the shoulder and played *Frogger* with the mad commuters just to salvage the SIM card. At least I could place it in her phone to let him know we were arriving. Most likely late, with this brilliant start.

Foolish as it was, and yes, risking road kill or DoD interrogation (those were the Bush years), it was all for naught. Nothing but. We decided to trudge toward the boonies with a wet printout, one hard head, a spurned ego, and two empty stomachs.

DC's grandeur gave way to the real America. Strip malls, rust belts, solitary spires of abandoned churches. Quite the opposite of home, where the better part of civilization lay beyond Mega Manila's histrionic streetlamps, soulless skyline, and in-your-face squalor. Ahead of us, the butt-nakedness of America said *howdy* as the trees shivered, and then the buildings came and stood few and far between. Diane was looking at the bottom of the page, now stained with cola and Frito grease. "We're close. Lehigh Valley," she said, as we turned on our last major highway into rural Pennsylvania.

The whole ride did make me question my sanity. Now over three hours on the road with yawning silences between Diane and me, and empty grey landscapes in between were enough for me to question why I was here to begin with. And what I gave up to come here. Not just this half-assed road trip, but the whole journey across the Pond. We joined a menagerie of 2nd-class citizens on the dole, bending over backward to get the A's, the brand-name diploma—the keys to the Kingdom—then the H1-Bs, and the almighty bungalow and picket fence, the blue passport and social security. Even if I was halfway toward my American dream and thinking of getting Diane to star in it, what I wanted at that moment was to just yank one of those white wooden stakes and to shove it up Uncle Sam's keister.

The snowfall was getting heavier against the stark plain. It might've been my hunger pangs, but I just imagined—wished for—that the frozen powder would turn into the sands of Boracay that I grew up with before the city slickers fucked it up beyond recognition. There, with a Guimaras mango smoothie and *kinilaw*, I used to hide behind my father's Ray-Bans and my swelling trunks as lobster-faced Scandinavians in their birthday suits walked knee deep in the shiny waters.

I sloshed upward trying to decipher the numbers by the porches of these creaky row houses. After the third, I walked up the steps. Number 18. No doorbell. I knocked. Then I called out. Nothing. *Just my luck; what will I tell Diane? It wasn't enough that I didn't give in last year when she asked; now I have nothing to show for it.*

The door creaked open. I was already panicking, but nothing prepared me for this welcome. Two large eyes scowled at me. I couldn't look away. After an interminable few seconds, I unfroze myself.

"What do you want, Mister!?"

As he stepped forward, the moonlight made him out to be more pitiful than gruesome. He looked like one of those severe Down Syndrome cases, but you could think worse in a place as unhinged as this.

"What is it, Charles!?"

A shadow rose from what looked like a couch and marched toward us.

I should either blurt something out or wet my pants.

"Mr. Grieger, I'm so sorry. I got lost on the way and didn't have my phone."

He looked at me astonished, as if he'd never seen anything but white skin in all his life. His hair was silver in the light, and his chin faintly traced by a Van Dyke beard. I braced myself, knowing there wasn't much to do but finish the job I started hours back.

"I was wondering if you'd ever come. Never mind...you're here, Son." He led me in and his companion shut the door behind me.

"You're a lot younger than I figured," he added, scratching his head as to how to explain his circumstances. *And darker*, I muttered under my misty breath. His TV was snowy and just bright enough to showcase the mess strewn about the den.

"Yeah, and I didn't want to trouble you sir, I'll be happy to pick up the cello so you can go back to bed." *Keep it proper and brisk, then get to business...*

"Ah, yes, the instrument. If you'll come with me down-stairs, I'll show it to you. The cello, right?"

No, the Lamborghini, you Redneck. I tried to contain myself and followed him anyway. Better than being left with Quasimodo. As we got off the last step, I now knew what he meant. From where I was just seconds back, I had stepped into a palace. The walls were bare, but immaculately white. The light was flickering, but it only added to the mystique. Hanging or leaning on them were all these vintage heirlooms. Trombones. Grandfather clocks. What looked like Flemish oil paintings. Violas, fugues, harps. In the dimness, a time warp of beautiful patina. It calmed and lulled me; I almost forgot about my companion parked outside the shack and on top of the ravine.

"Where did you find all these treasures?" I was astonished.

"Thank you, my friend. You see, my Church goes searching across these old towns to find them. We use them to keep our community alive."

Sounded noble enough, and what an *honest* living. As he disappeared from view to look into a smaller storage room, my eyes helped themselves and explored the room. There they were, mementoes of generations past, immaculately preserved, but for some dust. I had little time to spare, but pored over them every second he gave looking for my cello.

"How neat! Which parish is this?" Feeble small talk, and he didn't seem to hear me anyway. As I turned around, there was a place in the wall adorned with his own artifacts. The light was getting faint, but I could make the images out as I panned my eyes. In happier days, a photo of what looked like him, dark cropped hair embracing what I then made out to be his son, and a beautiful woman sharing the frame, but looking away. Then, the next one more recognizable; the two of them without her, and with both their features coming about. A few more to the right, and then my spine tingled. Amid the rustle of packages in the inner room, I walked toward the image that caught my eye. Unmistakable. Flames licking a beard. The gnarled ears, pointing to spiralled horns, framed by a crimson background. And eyes that still look at me when I close mine. In the backwaters of my country, with its surfeit of baby-eating *aswangs* and bat-winged *manananggals*, this still puckered the goose pimples on my hairless arms.

"Found it! Let me show it to you." I almost knocked over a lyre.

"Charles, get our friend here something warm to drink while I tune his instrument," he smiled as he dragged the black case toward me.

I reached into my pocket and grabbed it.

"Sir, no need for that!"

I thrust him with all I had (seven Ben Franklins, more than worth his trouble).

"But *Son*..."

"I have to go," I winced, as I pried the neck from his hands. "That should be worth the trouble."

As I swung toward the staircase, the cello's case toppled the grandfather clock and it tipped toward the massive collection. Grieg gave a short cry and leapt forward in vain to catch it. I stormed up, flailing in the dark hallway toward the doorknob reflecting the TV light, I heard a low groan as I clothes-lined his son out cold. The voice rose from the stairwell into the night.

"You'll regret this. We will find you. Damn you!!!"

I didn't stop to hear the rest even as they seemed to echo through the frozen air. I found the car door latch and yanked it open only to hear more screams. There was Diane, banging her palms and soles all over the dash...

"What the hell took you so long! I thought I heard something coming from below. Something's been moving over *there!*" She pointed with her suede-tipped fingers over to the ravine, along with her stuffy, reddish nose.

The Haunted Cello

I was in no mood to apologize, let alone get into a horror-story pissing contest. I hit the reverse, jammed the handbrake. We backed up all the way up the hill, my eyes just focused on the road. I swore I'd run over anything that tried to stop us. Diane's banshee backseat driver antics kept me sane until we crossed the tracks, and not once did I ever look back until we found the interstate.

"Turn the wipers on, you idiot!"

So much for the demure Filipina image I'd preserved all these years. And when I mustered enough sense to flick the switch to see how much of the flurries had come back, I knew we were coming home, cold and numb, but no longer hungry. The three of us. Then, as we reached the district, it was just me and my backseat passenger.

I only opened her up once. It was as advertised. Honey-coloured spruce and maple base, luthier's scroll signed in the hollow: perfect but for a tiny hairline crack. And who cared? Once I tried to get Fr. Walsh on the Hilltop to bless it with holy water, but he just told me I'd either been watching *The Exorcist* too many times, or spent too much time in the Third World. From a Jesuit who actually taught William Peter Blatty, what a hoot—although I did, on both counts.

In my country, everything from houses, to automobiles, to foreskin had to get christened, *at least every 6 years*. By the time I'd lugged the heathen in its case around M Street to find a cab that would take me, I just felt like crashing but stayed oddly alert. Couldn't afford a fourth sleepless night with it staring at me in my efficiency, like a casket waiting to creak open. So, I just took my grandmother's weapon of choice—*Dormicum*—and started to pass out.

I WOKE UP. It was mid-day. A text message from Diane. *Cryptic, but so good to hear from her.* I needed some contact, and besides, I never got to apologize. She said she believed my story, the one I catatonically ranted on in the car in broken *Tagalog* and crisp swearing. I agreed to meet her in my flat at four, just enough time for me to make it, and her, more agreeable. Two solid hours went by, which I spent blanching the peanut butter stains off the couch and collecting all the *Cheetos* and pizza crumbs and God knows what else was on the carpet. Then after indulging in another massive helping of Smuckers, I gave in to a nap.

It was dark when I woke up. *Dammit, I must've slept through her calls!* As I started patting around for the phone, I felt a heavy, cold grasp on my wrists. Brute force lifted me and flung me across the darkness. I could see how the street lamp eerily traced the broken furniture and my unwelcome guests around them. They were robed, hooded in what looked like blotched crimson. I heard a tortured scream downstairs as they began to close in on me. *Diane!* My throat strained, but no sound came out. I tried to reach out, but my limbs failed me.

In the lone shaft of moonlight, a chorus of pale-veined hands shot out from the robes and reached for my useless, catatonic arms and legs. In unison, the voices filled the room and took hold of my senses, as cold bony hands wrung my neck. As he removed his hood, Grieger's eyes were blood-red. He looked larger than when I'd left him, like the horde that stood behind him in the shadows. They swarmed around me, and before I could—like any cafeteria Catholic—make the sign of the cross and cough up a Hail Mary, I felt my lungs bursting as the many hands clenched tighter, blotting out my sight and breathing.

MY EYES OPENED AS I convulsed, in the middle of my screaming. I scratched the morning glory off and realized my limbs were back in service. I was drenched in tears, sweat, and a warm dribble of piss. It was bright outside. For a moment I thought I was back at my parents' house, feeling my way through the memories of another house party. But then my teeth began chattering, and my body went fetal. My eyes wandered around as I shivered and patted around for a comforter even as my tongue dried out from the futile heater. The flat was in the familiar happy mess that I, not they, had left it in.

The cello was still there, waiting for me, smaller, it seemed, in the sun's glare.

Dr. Kamrad's evening class was for today. I reached for my phone to check how much time I had. And still wish Diane had texted. *But of course!* All I had brought with me from that weekend was in chips and dross on frozen asphalt. I lost everything valuable except for the evil incarnate leaning against the closet, watching me.

I lugged it down the stairs, and didn't care for the bumps and cracks as I dragged it across the Key Bridge like Achilles' tenderized Hector. I thanked the sun, the lack of wind chill, and chapel spires on the hill ahead of me. I would finally go back to Mass tonight, lest my grandmother decided to come back to haunt me as well.

On the top of Prospect Street, in homage to my frocked forebears, and still in my PJs, I unleashed it from its box. In plain sight, I held it up with my hands, like a titan chokes a mortal dangling in mid-air. It was now unhinged, cracked at the bottom, but golden and helpless in the sun.

I heaved, then cast it down those Exorcist steps until it met the banks of the melting, rushing Potomac. My chapped lips kept me awake. I started looking beyond the beltway, pining for the warmth of sand, and my bare feet touching the water's edge.

Paracelis Goes to Baguio

PARACELIS BOARDS THE bus that will take her to Baguio. Baguio was the city of her dreams, because of what she heard from her mother.

Her mother's watch hung loosely on her wrist and told her it was 4 a.m., right on time for her to be picked up and accompanied below the village. The village was still asleep, including Grandmother who kissed her goodbye the night before. Before she left for the station with *Manang Gawani*, Paracelis gazed at everything around her, thinking it might be the last time she would see the place she'd grown up in. In the fading darkness, she made out the outlines of the laddered huts and thatched roofs for the last time.

Time was no match for Paracelis' expectations as she sat firmly in front of the bus, excited to be the first one to get on, then off. Off they went, past the last junction which met the village's dirt road. The village was hardly seen from the bottom, but as the driver picked up the pace to lead the bus down the valley, she could imagine Grandmother waking up, too late to wave—with tears. Tears were overshadowed by the embracing forest that grew smaller and smaller as the valley gave way to craggy rocks, ravines, and dry gorges.

The dry gorges were not there during her mother's time. Time had not been kind to the *Cordillerans*, with their welcoming of the lowlanders. Lowlanders and foreigners who professed 'modernization' that meant wealth for the miners and loggers who worked hard and ate well. Well enough to bring their large families up the mountains to take in the crisp air while they desecrated age-old forests, threw concrete at everything in their path, and blackened the waters and valleys.

Valleys that Paracelis no longer recognized as the bus made its way past the winding roads that grew wider and smoother, but led to harsher sights—hills increasingly pock-marked all over with shanties where the trees once danced with the wind. Winding down the road as she sensed she was near, Paracelis closed her eyes and thought: *"Maybe this is a test from Kabunian: 'the night is a dark blindfold worn before the daylight makes all things well again'* said her mother.

Her mother spoke of benevolent white men and even whiter cottages. Cottages where she cooked and cleaned for a widowed serviceman with whom she fell in love. Love that led to a child. A childbirth that led to death, a provenance that eluded Paracelis until her thirteenth birthday, one she dutifully celebrated with her grandma. Grandma felt it was time

to let her only granddaughter know about the truth, woven
with myth, but it would do:

"*Apo*, was Mother really taken from me by the white *anitos*,
and is this why my skin is so pale?"

"Pale—ha! Your mother left us early but that was her
sacrifice for your gift. She watches over you and loves you.
The *puraw anitos* have given you skin like pearls, whiter than
any of our people, an amulet that will help you move easily in
the world. It was even your mother who said so."

"So *Apo*, remember that story you told me about the spirits?
Will they help me now?" Now grandmother was already old,
and could not quite remember at first. First, she was angry,
for she rued the day she could no longer keep Paracelis at
home. Home to her was as fluid as her blood, running underneath her bright skin, bringing her to places where she would
pursue her adventure and life.

"Life has woven you an unfinished garment. While I do not
want you to go, you have been given another gift by the white
anitos and their priests, the *Episkopalyans* who will take care of
you in Baguio and then bring you to your father's world. The
world is harsh, you will see, but this village right now cannot
contain your spirit nor your mind, my beautiful child."

"Child!?" *Apo*, I will soon be a woman, and I choose to
leave with this gift, and that's all I've ever wanted, more than
this place could ever give."

"Give your people some respect, *Ading*. We are unlike
anyone in the world outside the village and soon you will see."

"See, *Apo*, you don't get it. Baguio is calling me and I cannot
wait to see the beautiful cottages, the beautiful clothes, culture,
and people. I want to be modern."

'Modern' was the word for Baguio. Baguio was the summer
capital of the *gringos*, the colonizers who drove off the *Kastilas*
and many of their friars before they could completely destroy
the indigenous culture of the Cordilleras as they did in the

lowlands. Lowlands that had already become a wasteland of urban blight, poverty, and despair.

DESPAIR WAS THE farthest thing from Paracelis' mind as she folded her woven clothes. Clothes that she was eager to replace with the outfits she saw in one of the magazines her mother had left behind, filled with foreign images so different from Paracelis' life in the village.

The village was dark when she went outside, shrouded in fog that brings *Gaddangs* their dreams. Dreams that stir the women to weave these visions through their backstrap looms. Looms that wrought the most unique and beautiful of tapestries—so mystically different, even among all the Cordillera tribes. Tribes that often fought and fought until their culture fell into decline. Decline that the Gaddangs, because of their isolation from the rest of 'civilized' and warring world, would avoid, so far.

So far were their villages that the Gaddang kept to themselves, fended for themselves, and learned to keep their traditions. Traditions that suffused every part of their life—invoked so viscerally by the women weavers into their cloth that physically had the same colour and fabric as the other tribes, but always with one thing more.

More than the warp and weft could do with dreams, the women weavers asked their families—their men, their elders, and their children—to bring them tokens to weave in them: bone, seeds, shells, magic beads, minerals and mementoes. Mementoes that now included Paracelis' mother's pearl earrings, given to her by the white *anitos*, or so her grandmother told her. Her mother's photograph, surreptitiously hidden in between pages of one of the magazines, betrayed the truth; for holding mother's hand but looking away was a milk-skinned man, and Paracelis often recognized his smile in the slowing brook whenever she washed her woven garments, all packed inside her basket, except the one she wore on the ride to Baguio. Baguio after all, deserved to receive her in her best self when she stepped onto the city. The city was 'sophisticated', and with her moonlit complexion and mystical attire she might still be able to impress her new guardians. Guardians who would teach her all the new things that might finally take her to her real father's home halfway around the world. The world was so big after all, and Paracelis felt her heart would beat large enough to contain it.

HER EYES WELLED UP from the soot of the diesel trucks that piled up as the city came into view for the first time. *Time must be such a cruel god*, Paracelis thought, as she saw for herself the city of her dreams. Dreams that bore no resemblance to the syrupy stories that Mother had told her as a little child. Children were running with dark, tattered rags, now coming up to the vehicles, speaking broken English and a dialect she could not comprehend; shouting curses when the drivers or passengers would ignore their cries, with their parents disappearing into the mines or the brothels that had sprouted like rings around this rotting trunk of Baguio.

Baguio looked cruel, lonely, and heart-breaking; and no amount of wishful defiance could convince her there was something better that lay beyond the poisoned hills before her. Her mental pictures of the white cottages, the benevolent white people, the happy homes, and blossoming garden lands were nowhere to be found.

Founded by the *Ibalois*, the *Gaddangs*' distant kinfolk, Baguio a generation ago, was exactly as her mother described and loved. Loved enough to forgo her beloved people and home. Home that she believed Paracelis would also leave one day.

Day announced its arrival through the warmth beginning to pierce the windows as the bus snaked its way through the red, carved mountains with her muted passengers. Passengers, a menagerie of bloodlines, were coming to life one by one. One of them, an *i-Kalinga*, set aside his miner's hat, stretched his dark, tattooed arm across the aisle, and tapped Paracelis on the shoulder.

ADING. MANGAN TAYON.

Paracelis' eyelids are heavy, but she manages to reciprocate. She nods, let his gnarled fingers and knuckles meet her forehead as a benediction to an elder. She can taste her bile from the twists and turns as her excitement waned with her vision. The fog of the early morning but an image in her head, and she feels a strange pain near her belly. Yet in those very seconds, as she traces the bone fragments in her shawl, she feels more serene than the reality outside the bus.

Agyamanak, apu, naimbag nga bigat. She tells the old warrior.

His other arm stretches out, revealing the painful etchings of his forebears. It reveals an unopened orange. She refuses, but he insists. His smile, like the sheared mountains, is red-stained with betelnut. They settle on her taking the peel, inhaling its goodness, and she leans her head back as he withdraws to his side and looks outward to the oncoming horizon.

Paracelis knows she is falling into the land of dreams and welcomes it as her elders taught her to.

She looks down at her arms and legs and can tell she is much older. She is standing in the mirror. Gone are the beads, and her hair is tied in their place, its tail peering from behind. Blue walls surround her—not like the sky's, but like those ponds that she sees near the mineshafts. She doesn't want to look at her face and instead turns around to find out where she is. There are books around her, but she cannot recognize nor understand the titles. She steps forward, struggling to reach the doorway. When she reaches for the knob, she pauses and tries to trace the grain on the door. But instead feels the coldness of the slab, unlike her village walls, where each plank retains its life as an offering to the gods for shelter. Little pictures on the wall catch her eye; she moves closer to examine them, almost with a blank stare. In one, she is veiled surrounded by blank, cold mountains. In the other, she is sitting down, surrounded by a white, curly orange-haired clan, almost pressed from all sides. Not unlike her father, Paracelis can barely look at her spouse's face. And at that moment, she fears he is on his way back to their house as the sun fades into the orb of the cobalt den.

She feels paralyzed, and wants to leave, but starts frantically looking about. There is a metal steamer trunk near the bed. She rummages through that, then rushes to the opened glass closet to run her hands through the long, shiny gowns, looking for the familiar texture of her missing, woven garments. She can feel nothing visceral in this place. She brusquely seals the cabinet, and suddenly, her mouth feels dry as she sees her reflection once more. Behind her, the redness of the horizon looms over the jagged shadows of the glassy towers. In this crimson back-drop, Paracelis sees her skin turn paler, like drying ivory, and slowly, she begins to feel her life draining.

HER EYES FLUTTER OPEN as she wakes to a strange sen-sation, almost like that of a rushing brook beneath her. Her nostrils pick up the scent of fresh blood, reminding her of the ritual preparations of each *kanyao* in her village, shaved sacrificial hogs, their jugulars opened to drain the unclean and bless the *dap-ay* soil. Soiled were her thighs, her seat dampened with her womanhood, and she misses her mother and starts to miss her. Her fresh woven cloth is all she has, and she takes it from the basket, using its deep red patterns to stanch her pelvis, thighs, and the remaining blood away.

Away beyond the blighted hills, and with her own rite of passage behind her, Paracelis did finally see a small green spot, with a rusted barbed wire fence surrounding it. It's as if these metal borders were the only things standing in the way of the rotting decay threatening to infect the tiny, lonely pine-shrouded hill that she was approaching.

Approaching the gate, the driver called, "This is your stop, *ading.* I will tell *Apo Bielmaju* you got in fine. Be good, and don't forget where you came from."

Don't forget where you came from—those words kept ringing in her ears, and as the bus swayed to a stop, the sound of her hanging beads rippled through the gated, silent hill and into the trees.

The trees rustled one by one downward, until a white man—not as divine-looking as she had imagined—stepped outside to greet her and take her hand. Her hands were pale, paler than her skin, but soon warmed to the touch of Reverend Peter. Reverend Peter's smile conquered any fear Paracelis had as they climbed up the steps.

"The steps are steep, dear, would you mind helping this old man up?"

Up the winding path they went, with Paracelis clutching the old man's arm, the other her reddened *tapis* skirt as she looked around her new home. Her new home, the *Episkopalyan* School, was run by the Reverend's wife Linda, who met the two of them at the threshold and walked them through the blooming gardens. Gardens that led them to a white cottage, and when they inside, she gave her a warm hug, tighter than her mother or grandmother had ever tried in the past.

Past the bookcases, through the fireplace, and into a brightly-lit room, Paracelis was led and left there by Linda until they would serve supper with the other students. Students, she thought, who must be as lonely as her; but instead, all she could hear were songs and laughter. The laughter that suddenly reminded her of the village children, so different and yet so much a part of her.

Her fingers traced the beads of her skirt and palmed the pearls her mother and father had left behind. Behind her was a long journey; ahead, an uncertain way, she thought as she sat down to unpack her things and for the first time smiled through her tears.

Deep South

I SPENT A DRUG LORD'S fortune on the Azkals.

It was the World Cup qualifiers at Panaad. Christmas carols being sung by the fans. A freak cold front from the Marianas had blown into port, enveloping the sugar fields around us. It marched past the stadium lamps and through my scrubs, nipping at my balls and raising the few, fine hairs I had on my limbs.

Actually, it was more than that.

Xiang Qiang and his band of coolies were on their way to
collect, and I had to go for broke. They'd been lenient until the
big crash, when his poor wife—the one with the third nipple
and lightning reflexes—placed a bet on PLDT stock just before
the ZTE merger fell through.

I took a cue from her *chutzpah*, with a difference.

I believed in the striker.

All Harry Platypus needed to do was listen to his devout
mother's strictures and father's Saxon cabbie instincts to make
that penalty and even the score. Well, the more gifted of the
mongrel twins conveniently caught chlamydia from a Thai
cheerleader in last week's friendlies, and was now hobbling
on the big day—my big day. A draw was enough for my bookie
and my life, and it was slipping away in front of me.

All eyes were on Harry—as his fingers kept raiding his
crotch area for all to see on the big screen by the cheap seats—
right where the ball, guided by Harry's wayward balls, landed.
Congratulations, Burma. Just over a decade of freedom, and
you've now kicked our asses in everything. Uniforms included:
at least yours are original.

The fans trudged out like a funeral march, while the team
did their obligatory lap. This time, no one, not even Gordon
– who by now hated his older-by-six-minutes brother for the
endorsements and skanks he was getting—went to hug him.

I needed one.

Well, I did get one when the team Muse (groupie) rushed at
me, crying no doubt from groin burn. Prying myself from her
liposuctioned arms, I told her I'd have a look in the morning
and write out a prescription. Chances are, it's just bacterial;
a couple of weeks she can snog again with the rest of them.
Gynaecology is an acquired specialty, by way of the occasional exploration and *labiaplasty*.

THESE DAYS I DON'T even know what kind of practice I really run. Back at the office, my walls are peppered with citations and post-grad training at King's and Cal, satellites revolving around the honours degree from the State U. At the rococo waiting room, Jam, my virginal receptionist (the lone *Ilongga* member of the Mocha girls), now reconfigured, lay waiting to flatter the regulars and charm their benefactors, always ready to put out. My mentor's rule was 'You don't lay where you stitch,' so I never really indulged. Somehow she didn't cut it for me anyway.

My office doubled as a recovery room, where I liked watching my patients, sedated and swollen like Frankenstein's bride, peacefully heal until the anaesthesia wore off and they terrorized the community again. Behind me stood two mementoes to my current and former life: my BenCab painting and my Bee Gees lunchbox. To my left, a bedroom doorway, and in it, a futon, my Kindle Fire 12.0 charger, and a safe. I didn't do credit and they really wanted to pay in cash, never mind the provenance. All in all, enough to run a respectable operation.

Well, at least until now.

The pad is niftily tucked away on the cove across Pacific Shoals, a shiny, neo-Mediterranean gated community in Talisay. The subdivision looked like a Klingon spaceship that landed on a swamp, with the swamp threatening to claw its way back, like the jungle of Angkor Wat. *No offense meant to the Khmers.* This backwater town would've stayed that way if it weren't for the squatter colonies driving out the middle class from claustrophobic Bacolod down South; and, coming the other way, the younger families sick and tired of their crazy cousins' drive-by coke wars in old, rotting Silay. A perfect location. Just down the highway, a constant bevy of shrivelled-up housewives from Santa Clara Village sneaked in for their quarterly botox jabs. Even nearer, right across the new highway, a tricycle ride for the nostril-envy *queridas* of Anvaya North Point for their weekly glutathione IV fix and complimentary sunscreen.

Once in a while on a good harvest and if the *haciendero* felt like it, we'd get lucky enough to plug silicone on these tarts from as far away as passé Iloilo and God-awful Cebu. Even Harry, Gordon, and the rest of the mongrels pumped my revenue stream. After the Azkal-mania hit the archipelago and the airwaves, I started getting more quiet visits from the *balikbayan nouveaux riches*, pining to look like the half-breeds, and my patient ratio of males/queens to women almost evened out. In the span of six months with ABS-CBN's coverage of each football match, the Rhino-Gluteal-Glutathione (RGG) package was born. Jam's task was to chat up the rest of the *chavs* at Pacific Shoals and give them a discount. She even came up with the idea of bundling in sublets in their kitschy McMansions. We'd offer them for convalescing clients who didn't want to be spotted at the airport or on Lacson Street, where everyone tries to hide in plain sight anyway.

With the parched haciendas giving way to the new airport, I made a great bet on this place when I set out from Imperial Manila six years ago. But that's all I can say for my luck these days.

Last April, as Iñaki walked through the door, I knew I was in for shit. The man-child didn't need any retooling, and he went past Jam without a wink. He sported his father's Basque profile, and a frame built to mount a horse, along with the floozies he brought home from Cebu in his powerboat. Like the Playtpi/podes, he inherited nothing physically from his mother. No one ever questioned Doña Nena's provenance, a dusky *morena*, a convent-schooled but seminary-bred lass whose uncanny knack for handicrafts and cost accounting all but saved their family from the last commodity crash. Her family, the notoriously-incestuous Mondillos, frittered away most of their holdings after a generation of 'keeping it in the family.' Her mother's weekly confessions and private penance with an Augustinian in old Jaro actually saved that part of the clan, and with her chance meeting with Don Javier Zabalona at a soiree with St. La Salle, it set them back toward genetic redemption.

Well, almost.

"*HIJO DE PUTA*, DOC!"

"What's up *cabron*?" my knee-jerk response kicked in as I reconciled last month's overhead.

"Daddy's lost his marbles." And here I thought I'd seen the last in-bred sob story.

"The fucking *Gringos* pulled the plug on us—no more fucking sugar quota, *punyeta!*"

"I heard. What does that have to do with me?"

"I'm getting cut off. With that stupid Brexit happening again, Mommy's selling the house in Playa de la Concha, and the Jag I was supposed to get at 30."

"And...?" Iñaki's narcissism and his withdrawal symptoms were simply indistinguishable.

"Be my partner, *coño*. We'll start tonight. My dealer's boating into town." He was talking to me as if he was pre-bludgeoned Dickie Greenleaf and I, the ever-besotted Tom Ripley. "You fix him up. It'll be easy—he doesn't wanna look *guapo*, like me. Just different." Always such a tease when he wanted something.

"No sweat," I said, "we just have to detox him before he goes under." It wasn't my first express surgical disguise case, but this was a heavy hitter, and then some.

"That's not all. If the *pendejo* comes out fine, he'll leave his stash with us until he gets back from Xiamen at Christmas. When he leaves, we launder and skim."

It's hard to tell which hallucinogen was kicking in this time, since he had started on the hard stuff months back. I myself tried everything I prescribed to his brat pack, and nothing ever made me this antsy.

I was more than intrigued, if honoured, at the offer.

All this time I'd never been one of them. My ancestors came over through a land bridge, not a galleon. I went to Philippine Science High School, where herded nerds plotted socio-economic vengeance amid another cleared plantation-turned-complex in good old Panay.

In reality, it was my location, and his own shame—more than my lineage—that led Iñaki to me.

I was now a fart's stench away from the drop-off point.

XIANG QIANG'S NARCO-SUB emerged just outside the cove, and the flashing green light from its conning tower looked more and more like my favourite scene from *Gatsby*, even more now that we were bootlegging, too. *Strange consolation*. Iñaki and I took his speed craft, *El Carajo*, and we killed the motor as we floated toward the sub. Out from it emerged a silky pair of legs slicing through a *cheongsam*, a deadly grace interrupted moments after by a rough clanging sound of belted girth extricating itself from a porthole.

"Mr. Qiang." Iñaki bowed as he steadied the boating ramp to let them through. I was panting and looked around us for any sign of the Coast Guard, but knew it was just the munchies: our beloved Armed Forces would just as come near the Spratlys than spot us under a full moon in sleepy Negros Occidental.

"It's Xiang! The first name goes after. Can't you ever get it right?"

"Too much product. Sorry, Su—I mean, Yin."

Su Yin, the dealer's manager-mistress, removed her veil and leered at me, although with the moonlit sky she could've just been squinting. I could fix that as well if she wanted. Half the Korean community in Bacolod can swear to it with open eyes.

"Is this the Doctor?" She gave same look at my *mestizo* companion. I felt relieved.

"Yes. He's the best bang for your *yuan*. "

"It's *renminbi*, you cokehead. Is he ready to do this!?" Mr. Qiang looked perplexed and famished from the trip and the pre-op protocol.

"Yes, Ma'am!...Same difference, *de puta madre*." Iñaki muttered as the engine roared and we slid into the clinic's back entrance.

"Does he have anything in his system? I have to know, Ma'am." From my *pangga*'s stories, the only thing she had in common with the Mainland wife was that they loved to starve him 'til they got what they wanted.

"The trick to a fortune, Doctor—what's your name?—is you don't quaff what you sell. He's clean."

"It's Dr. Anacleto...Jim." I offered to shake her hand, but she sneered at me again this time, still no eyeballs in sight.

MY SURNAME DOESN'T give me much more than a raised eyebrow in these parts.

My parents were former OFWs turned Baptist missionaries from Ilocos Norte. They were amongst the last of the Rockefeller grantees sent to convert the rest of the dregs in the Visayas that the Archdiocese didn't bother with once they had secured the *buenas familias*. Between their chosen careers and hidden dreams, I was fucked from the start. Father was a seaman turned assistant salon manager who met my tertiary nurse mother at a pre-departure orientation during the first labour exodus in the mid-'70s. She's long gone now, but I wanted to make her proud by taking her field a few notches higher. Papa, who now runs the Scissors Palace franchise in sleepy Batac, has quite a following—dispensing Omani proverbs and leaflets with *New and Improved Pagoda Cold Wave* lotion and highlights to his clientele—and to me, via prepaid SMS. I've tried to run away from his legacy, only to keep running into it when I fulfilled Mama's. You never kick the habit, I guess. His last monthly message read: *El Helou Bi Shoof El Helou.* [1] I could relate, and that's why I make 'em beautiful just the way I see it.

After Science High and a sleepy bout of B.S. Biology in Dumaguete, I nailed a scholarship at the State Med School on Taft Avenue. I must admit, the alphabetical roll calls served me well when they looked for interns, just as it did after on the yellow pages and HMO lists when I started my practice.

Manila those days was already the dung heap it is now, and I lived right under the city's armpit while doing my residency. But when I'm buggered out, I often think about one of my patients, and found it strange that he came to mind as I watched Xiang and his paramour disappear into the sub, which vanished into the now-moonless sea.

THE OPERATION WAS a success. We didn't recognize him from Mao. Even Su Yin left smiling with the collagen jab I tossed in for free, and they left us with 86 kilos of nose candy and crisp, recently converted greenbacks, for safekeeping.

---

[1]   Only the beautiful see the beautiful.

Iñaki was a hapless plodder, but he sure could sell the stuff and earn enough trust for the arrangement. After all, he was one big node in an intermarried set of *hacenderos*—whose dozens of scions had the neurological bent to be hooked on the product—until they passed it on to the next inbreeds who'd have nothing left but the habit and a host of less subtle deformities.

"You got da bezt mah-ket in the wowld. We'z gonna be in bizness looong taym!" Xiang kept repeating as he stuttered through the sedatives.

My new 'partner,' true to his class, took all the blow and left me with half the Benjamins.

"We've got five months, *pangga*, use it, don't lose it."

AS THE LIGHTS DIMMED in the stadium, I rushed toward the Gullwing to make it back to the flat. With thoughts of Su Yin slicing my nuts for Xiang's congee, I remembered Datu Jiz again, and it finally hit me.

I WAS ON THE LAST year of my residency, on my midnight shift at the second-floor burn unit. Everything was so still you could hear a cockroach take a dump. Amid the smell of skin grafts on melted flesh, a new patient got wheeled in. This one was different. The man kept shouting, not with the pain, but the right to keep his *taqiyah* on.

"Wasalam alaykum." I managed to get it right. *Thanks, Pa.*

"Alaikum assalam." He smiled.

How the simplest gestures can open up a whole world.

Having just ended a sparkless relationship with a *kolehiyala*, I had all the time to chat him up. Through his stoic recovery,

Datu Jiz told me everything—from how his uncle, the Rajah Muda, slept day in and out in a tiny apartment, pining for the glory days of his Sultanate, while his illegitimate toddlers from his *muchachas* ran amok past the cracked, green linoleum. He also told me how he ended up here (burning his arms after trying to flambée a manta ray's tail).

Datu Jiz refused plastic surgery, thinking this made him look more like the Tausug warriors of old; I must say he was right. Nobody wanted to mess around with a six foot, *kris*-wielding man with gnarled, striated forearms and flaring nostrils. Over the weeks as his grafts dried up, I would come by the Malate apartment to replace the bandages. I would also do the odd basic bits for the Royal Family—titled and all, but broke in everything, including the hygiene department. After curing the Rajah Muda of the ringworm that made him look like a rabid zombie, I was treated like one of their own.

On my off-duty hours, I'd walk across the hospital and into M.H. del Pilar Street, past the brothels and shawarma stands to fetch halal starch and join them for a humble feast. In between that final year and the time I set up shop in narcissistic Negros, they were my family, waiting for me to sit at their feet after a meal of turtle eggs, *curacha, samaral,* and other goodies smuggled in by their subjects from the peninsula in their Deep South.

One night, after a pack of contraband *Gudang Garam,* Datu Jiz motioned for their entourage to leave the room so it was just me and the Crown Prince.

"Doc—when the tides turn and you have nothing more to prove, you will have a place waiting for you with your brothers in Simunul."

"With a wife waiting?" I found myself an extra shot of chutzpah after my fourth turtle yolk, playing with the crumpled *ping-pong*-like shells as we sat on the rug and our eyes traced the *hookah* smoke.

"How many did you want, my friend?" Datu Jiz volleyed back.

"We'll even supply the dowry, in exchange for lifetime care of our people, when I am Sultan." Rajah Muda hollered from across the room, as he stroked the hair of one of his poor heirs.

"I would be honoured, Your Highness, maybe one day. *Insha Allah.*"

ONCE MY PRACTICE TOOK off, I barely kept in touch, except for the odd news on the Sultan's cancer prognosis as the government kept them at bay on their territorial claims, and stood by the Malaysians. But I always had the coordinates and the Datu's mobile number locked in the safe with my crumpled pesos and Xiang's greenbacks that I blew on that diseased penalty kick.

Iñaki, that lovely bastard, could never handle his coke, let alone his cash.

MONTHS AFTER THE SUB departed, I had the urge to drive to Murcia and his parched hacienda to try to collect the proceeds before he and his ilk squandered all of it.

Well, he used his share of the dollars to raze over 10 hectares worth of sugarcane. On that scorched loam he set up an astroturf polo field, with the sign 'New Alabang', after the Club that kicked him out for knocking up the manager's daughter.

As I drove in and peered across the field, I saw only a few bags left on a banquet table by the sidelines. It almost looked like the markers were made of blow. I hoped not, but that would have been easier to retrieve than a body cavity.

"I like what you did with the place!" I sneered as the horses brayed and he and his more inbred cousins charged about.

"Watch me *pangga*, I'll score one for you this last *chukker*." From afar I swear I could see his almost-aquiline nose, swollen red from Xiang's product. I walked a healthy distance from the boys and their steeds, while the prolific *sakadas* who helped clear the sugar canes stood by with their offsprings, clapping out of sync.

"*Oye*, Paco, I'm coming to get you!" He stabbed the horse with his heels as it galloped forward in pain.

As he raised his tight arse from the saddle to take a swing with his mallet, I saw him stiffen up like a white cock on blue pills. I knew in that split second, prolonged in my mind, that he'd gone up to meet Jesus.

I thought to myself: What a way to go.

His body was so rigid his hand didn't let go—even after his corpse dangled from the stirrup, as the horse chased after the wooden ball. The cousins sniggered and played on, oblivious and stuffed to the gills with Chinese snow, while my dear friend looked like Hector tenderized on astroturf.

When they finally came to, all they did was scream.

"*Putang ina*, Doc, fix him up, *coño*!" Caloy kept screaming, eyes red and mouth almost frothing. I looked at the pale, garnished corpse, and i bothered to take his pulse anyway.

While Paco and his cousin-uncle hugged and wept, I took Iñaki's keys as I gazed at the outline of his jodhpurs, and tried remembering his face underneath all the oozing lacerations. All he had left of any worth was docked outside my clinic, but I had to be sure.

I called the Zabalona residence and after the 12th ring, the servant answered. Since it took one to know one, she decided from my tone to give me the shrill, pidgin auto-response:

"Senyor Hab-yer y Senyora Nenita are een Madreeth, pobrecito. No se kung san-o sila mapuli diri!" then she slammed their brass receiver.

I shook my head from the impact and found Paco and Caloy staring with me with dilated pupils, too dehydrated to cry. "I'll go get an ambulance." I said dryly—and called the narcs, too—to stick it to the brats. Call it scorched earth, but I didn't want to touch the powder so I left it there for evidence, and thought I'd make it up on my terms at a sport I knew better.

LEAVING PANAAD STADIUM, with 43 missed calls from the bookie, and before I shut my phone off, I called Jam to meet me at the office. Xiang had all the law enforcers and immigration officers in his pockets, and once I traded the dollars myself it would be only hours before they'd serve me up on a plate for the gooks.

"Jam, Diin Ka Na? Magkadto ka na sa klinika."

"Sir—eh, diri na ako..." I should've known she took home a guest. I just hoped it wasn't a policeman.

"Ah, ganun, lihog siling palangga mo, magkadto na siya." I had no more time for staff feedback.

I almost maxed out my credit cards filling petrol containers and sunscreen at the Phoenix-CNOOC gas station, while downloading the entire *Paris Review* bestsellers' list and *Lancet* journals on my Kindle. I wasn't keen to leave a trace, but I wasn't going to a remote island without sustenance and tools. The Omron machine started spewing out the charge slips as both the *Santo Niño* and obese Buddha smiled down at me from the proprietor's crammed, plastic altar.

Local son and stubborn legend Joe Mari Chan's eternal ditty, "Christmas in Our Hearts," looped on and on as I gazed at the shiny, Guangdong-made Gautama's belly and I made one final indulgence. I tossed in a few purple peso bills for a bundle of *chicharon* to tide me over the nine-hour journey, just enough to cast off the packaging and any traces of pork rinds before I reached the Sultanate's outpost.

Even as I arrived to the scent of spunk, Jam redeemed herself. In under 15 minutes, she packed my accoutrements, the prescription pads and every drug I ordered into the trunk, and daintily wrapped and lay the BenCab and Bee Gees into it like corpses to a casket. I was a wreck: my hands, usually steady with surgical incisions, couldn't get the combination right for several minutes.

I gave Jam a hundred thousand pesos, with a promise to give her thrice the amount if she kept the Gullwing hidden at her diabetically-blind mother's—and the equipment, clinic, and my whereabouts under lock and key. She could use it as her love nest for all I cared, for as long as she cleaned up and paid the property taxes whenever—if ever—I returned.

The rest I told Datu Jiz I'd give for the *dowry*, and for my own cottage by the nearby islet off Simunul that the Rajah Muda described. *I think he might ask for the boat.*

During the occasional text banter, and when I called him this time, Datu Jiz sounded like my dad to me: *Inta Ghaleh Wa Talabak Rkhees.* [2] The best one I'd heard so far. He put me on speaker and the gruff, happy voices all told me to get my *halal-ified moreno* ass to come over.

I DON'T KNOW IF IT was what the Crown Prince described, or my desperate conjuring, but I easily imagined myself on the islet as *El Carajo* roared into high gear and the open sea:

---

[2]   You are precious to me and your request is cheap.

At the northern tip of the island, a newly groomed cottage by the ridge, straddling two crater lakes waiting over a hundred feet below. One, almost cobalt with salt water, the other, fresh and velvety dark. Both with depths unknown, filled with strange edible creatures and untouched by the islanders.

I imagined my new home, where I would return after attending to the Sultan's massive family and retinue. The cottage is small but open. Two windows would welcome the world in; one to face the virgin jungles at sunrise; the other, the open sea at dusk, with perfect circles of water, and their reflections inviting me in.

Every day, a fresh catch from the servants, and I could carve them up into fillets with a solar-powered cooling storage I'd smuggle in from Borneo through *El Carajo*, along with a year's worth of Arabic-lettered consumer goods. In the bedroom, waiting for me, would be one of the fairer, dark-lashed daughters of the last Arab merchant settler, beholden to the royal family and good enough for my blood, if not my appetites.

THE POWERBOAT'S GPS egged me to turn starboard, and I obliged as I savoured the last crackle of pigskin while looking at my iPhone. No more bars. I was out of coverage area, and finally on my own. I forgot to text Pa, as I thought of him missing Mama but enjoying his new encounters. His favourite sheik advice never left me: *When shopping, explore every tent in the bazaar.* I wish I remembered it in Arabic because it sounded so riveting, and thinking about my frustrating, dead *mestizo*, I was so close.

It was then the better of me crowded my thoughts as that nauseating refrain from "Christmas in Our Hearts" churned gleefully in my head.

Let's sing Merry Christ-mas,
And a Happy Holi-daaay,
This Season may-we-never-forget
The Love we-have-for-Jee-zus

May He be the One to guide us
As another New Year Starts
And may the Spirit-of-Christ-mas
Be Al-ways in Our Hearts...
...Aaaand may the Spirit of Christ-mas
Be Al-waaays
iiiin....
Ourrrr
Heaaaarts....

Possibly the worst-ever curse for Last Song Syndrome. *Christ*, I should've loaded up on i Tunes. Years would pass, and I'll find myself humming this garbled cheese—no Wi-Fi and Spotify for miles-with a *fatwah* around the corner. I looked up at the crescent moon, forgave that irony, too, and tried to focus on the bright side as the waves steadied along *El Carajo*'s charted path.

For a moment, I felt almost like Rizal settling in Dapitan. A happy exile with his *Moorish-Malay* Josephine Bracken, manly enterprise, and private practice lying in wait. Except that I wasn't a true physician; and I found it hard to call myself a man. He had two novels, a horde of women, and a revolution behind him. I had an overloaded, overpriced tablet, unrequited love for a pulseless cokehead, and a humourless Caliphate ahead of me.

The *Moros*, while sworn to protect an ally, would never let him out, either. Eventually, my new wife would squeal to her trader kinsmen about my ambivalence. The whole town, already nonplussed with my set-up, would soon figure out where I swung. Eventually, Rajah Muda would be left with no choice but have me hogtied and sent off to the Abu Sayyaf, and I'd lose the only thing I'd saved up—for a flaccid, stiffening corpse—to these uncut militants.

Then again, I could grow into my new life. I could store a few coconuts under the hut and ferment them into bootleg *tuba* for me and the restless islanders. Maybe spread the trade as far as Sandakan—if the Malaysians finally forgave us for invading Sabah. Or, just simply settle in. Bear a son with Yasmin, and set him straight in more ways than one. Grow old and forget the life I'd left behind and never belonged to anyway. Grow careless in my stride, inebriated, having nowhere else to go but walk into the sunset, over the crags, and fall head first into the lake and never come up for air.

I couldn't help but smile as the nautical twilight unsheathed the dark, nearing shoreline.

What a way to go.

October 2017

Antidote

"More than colour and forms, it is sounds and their arrangements that fashion societies. With noise, it is born disorder and its opposite: the world. With music is born power and its opposite: subversion. In noise can we read the codes of life, the relations among men."

—Jacques Attali,
Noise: The Political Economy of Music

MAVI SNAKED IN and out of the Halloween break hordes that trooped to Cloud 9, brandishing their selfie sticks like brooms. Quite a few of them, fresh from the airport and the Lazada 11-11 sale were already unleashing their fledgling drones like Quidditch snitches.

She shook her head as the cacophony of smartphone play-lists drowned out the surf. She climbed to the highest view deck where there was no cell signal, just pure air, and gazed at the kaleidoscope of surfers on their boards below. *They look like Spartans on their shields,* she thought to herself, as she gazed from the wooden structure, then zoned out and tried to let the swell and sea air fill her nostrils.

Mavi looked at her forearms and shins. They were peeling from the fortnight she'd already spent here. Uncle Joric, her *ninong* and legal guardian, had interceded for her temporary release from the facility and into his care.

"The sea can cure most anything if you just let Her," he had told his *inaanak*, as he packed her bags and sent her off on her own, knowing all too well she could have a relapse. He had decided, with the impulse of trust, to risk leaving her to the raw mercy of the elements, and the possibility that she might not even board her return flight once summer ended. But, after five years of on-and-off episodes, her organs saturated with chemicals, her mind numbed from the meds, he thought he'd chance it.

"For good measure, take this; and try to leaf through one a day." It was his flat-signed copy of Wendell Berry's *The Peace of Wild Things* that she had once read as a child, visiting his library on the weekends her parents gallivanted and left her to her own devices, one day never to return. There, she and her *ninong* would quietly sit in separate corners, with the sunlight streaming in as he edited his manuscripts and illuminating her first encounter with poetry.

It was a book her fingers often splayed open to land on Mr. Berry's verses—words she loved, before she even understood them, like the elements they belonged to. Then, sadly forgot once her teenage years, the city's entropy, and mobile phones took over.

This book she brought with her, crammed into a swollen backpack. Uncle Joric, in a rare intrusion, had curated the contents of the sack, allowing for his spare analogue Motorola, the meds she would soon be weaned off, a few modest bathing suits, her old flip-flops, several undies, tampons, and a few lubricated rubbers ("You never know, *Anak*"). She'd also brought a slim envelope he'd given her when she boarded the plane for Del Carmen.

Before allowing Mavi this fourteen-day birthday furlough, her counsellor had warned Uncle Joric to make sure she stayed off digital, her gateway addiction, and her *ninong* had promised that he would keep an eye on her always. He nodded, smiled at the shrink—and in his own terms, let her fulfil his commitment.

Mavi waited until the last surfer had paddled his way to the shore, as the sky's embers faded and the tides flowed in. On cue, the daily brownout foisted by the electric cooperative kicked in: the distant roar of the island's generators, the waves, and wind took over her senses.

As the motley crowd thinned, the magic-hour light for taking selfies and groupies fading, Mavi sighed and looked back towards the shore, trying to forget how she had to extricate herself the other night from a scruffy group of unkempt, overstaying Caucasians. Not because she didn't want to—she had often indulged in these things before life in the facility—but because she couldn't bring herself to feel a thing.

She smirked as they made a beeline to the shore, like winged insects towards the flickering of reggae music and strobe lights, taking with them their gadgets, gossip, their body odour that smelled of burnt crayon.

With that entropy behind her, she fell into the evening's embrace under the sheltering sky, and severed the last electronic leash. The Motorola was steadily beeping with birthday greetings from friends, undeterred by a sealed FB wall and dormant IG page, as well as from those who had bothered to send an SMS through Uncle Joric's number.

Mavi suddenly remembered his letter and she fished this from her bag, *na parang hinugot sa pwet ng kalabaw* as he would fondly christen their shared ADD symptoms growing up. Unable to make out the chicken-scratch writing on the creased paper, she folded it instead into a makeshift book-mark and promised to read it tomorrow, or at least on the plane back, she smirked.

Moonlight pierced the clouds, dimming the stars, as Mavi inserted the letter-cum-bookmark between the pages of Berry's book, prying it open. The letter-cum-bookmark landed on a short poem, heavily underlined, at the bottom of the dog-eared page. With her fingers, she tracked the letters like she once tracked the constellations on the night sky in her childhood.

Once there was a man who filmed his vacation.
He went flying down the river in his boat
with his video camera to his eye, making
a moving picture of the moving river
upon which his sleek boat moved swiftly
towards the end of his vacation. He showed
his vacation to his camera, which pictured it,
preserving it forever: the river, the trees,
the sky, the light, the bow of his rushing boat
behind which he stood with his camera
preserving his vacation even as he was having it
so that after he had had it he would still
have it. It would be there. With a flick
of a switch, there it would be. But he
would not be in it. He would never be in it.

Antidote

Mavi smiled as the clouds swallowed the moon once more. The winds carried a brief interlude of rain into the unwalled sanctuary. As the droplets began tickling her face, she opened her mouth and let out her tongue—not reluctantly this time, as she would with the Ritalin cocktails. The numbness gave way to the taste of brine; and memories, unadorned and unburdened, flooded in.

In that unfiltered moment, she closed her eyes and embraced everything, her senses approaching the waves in epistolary sequence.

Eulogist

SHE DESCENDS like snow into Dupont Circle North station.

The stone etching overhead has greeted her many times. But only now does she recognize it, her eyes frozen on the last three lines. As she disappears into the cavern, her neck arches backward; her ungloved fingers try to reach out to trace the words to chisel them into the memory of feeling.

> *...The hurt and wounded I pacify with soothing hand,*
> *I sit by the restless all the dark night—some are so young;*
> *Some suffer so much—I recall the experience sweet and sad...*

Her Metro card, down to the last quarter, is folded and creased. The machine mercifully accepts it as the jangling keys mingle with her last few dimes and nickels. Her hands fumble to feed the terminal. Her palms start rapping the cold metal face, as the grumbling queue grows behind her. The analogue screen reads 2.75. Barely topped up, the card is spit out. Just enough for this time, she says to herself.

Shady Grove. 22 minutes

NO RUSH. She is in the belly of the capital, and far away from home. Around her she notices the honeycomb arches, the waiting passengers, the vapours—all in sharper detail. A few paces away, a blind man is humming, tapping his cane on the cold, muddied floor. It is a familiar hymn, but she can't place it: *one that belongs to happier times*, she sighs.

She takes out her tablet—one of the few things the Paper left her as severance—and starts jotting. Her gaze wanders across the rail lines as her mind goes back to just a few hours ago. Back up the escalator, past the lifeless call boxes that emit nothing but static sparks to grazing limbs. Back into Kramer's, and its warmly lit nooks. She had walked into the 24-hour bookshop the night before; and, 'til dawn, rekindled her weekend postgrad ritual. Back when a midnight tryst at the 18th Street Lounge across the fountain was washed down with a pilgrimage to the only clean, *well-lighted place* in the Beltway.

Spanning two shifts, two men at the till cast sneers her way as she unhinges the inventory on the narrowed nooks of **Classic Fiction: F to M.** She finds the old Scribner's edition, the one with the art-deco dust jacket and the womb-like eyes piercing through the velvet Jazz Age night. She nests on the carpet until the streetlights gave way to dawn.

It's time. She makes her way through the ripples of shelves, wary of the leering vendor. He has just settled into his shift; one of those pale, veiny-armed bohemians that only made time for conversation with well-heeled, white patrons. She stops at the counter.

"Can I *now* help you, Ma'am?" He smirks and tries to stare her down.

"Yes, you *may*, Sir." She looks back up, indignant.

"Will that be *all*?" He raps his fingers on the glass case.

She points at the find. "Yes, but if you *look* at this jacket, it's stained and even torn."

He grabs the book from her, and rolls his bespectacled eyes. "We don't sell books in *that* condition. Did *you just*..."

"I am not going to put up with this..." She tiptoes and leans forward as the clerk shirks backward, bumping the register.

Behind her, a few of the nocturnal pilgrims bearing their own loot gather around and start to look over her shoulder.

"OK, Ma'am, if you'll be *kind* enough to get another one back there, we'll be over and done with." His eyes strain upward, trying to avoid the growing stares and mumbles.

She clears her throat, and lets her strength out. "No—you go back there and *fetch* me another one, or you give it to me at $12!"

She slams the hard-bound *Gatsby* on the counter with all her honour. He notices the corrugated flesh on her wrist; then after a few seconds, the faces now crowding around them.

"*Okay*, Ma'am. We can do that. Will you *still* be needing a bag?"

She sifts through the last slivers of fading green from her mottled billfold, now left with clipped, lifeless cards, and a faded press pass, memorials to her *life* in the main. She clutches at the volume, looking at the crimson flooring and exhaling as she exits, her breath turning to mist.

Red line. Doors Closing. Next stop, Woodley Park.

THE TRAIN BEGINS to break free of the city's embrace.
Inside, the chamber glows with a faint and sacred ordinary of
the city's margins. On the farthest seat there is a nurse, looking
away, fighting tears. Nearer, another defeated man, with the
stench of gin and gangrene wafting through the aisles. There
is plenty of space about the car, but she is too tired to move
away, pays no mind, and hunkers down.

Her writing goes on. She is trying to cobble together verses
before daylight:

> *When the mist meets your warmth*
> *takes your thoughts*
> *and turns them to tears*
> *Push off: your bed*
> *is a glass-bottomed boat*
> *and with your*
> *mahjong strokes*
> *wave then wander*
> *into a place*
> *where touch is*
> *what rekindles a smile,*
> *a promise; a brief reunion*

Van Ness-UDC. Tenleytown. Friendship Heights.

THE STOPS RING OUT in cold cadence. Fewer souls board
the train each rung out of the beltway. Hers and a crossing
trains have stalled in the station, longer than the usual pause.
Across, she espies the other coach, before it speeds off in the
other direction. It is filling up—most of them young, their
heads filled with ambition, bodies fermenting with caffeine,
and the dregs of last night's antics. There is a soldier standing

at attention, trying not to gaze downward at the Congressional aide he has given his seat to. The staffer stares blankly as he struggles for a line. Behind the seat, another waif, possibly a K Street intern, pats her bangs and seems to let out a huff as she finds herself next to an *imam*, his eyes closed and fingers parsing his wiry beard, lips moving with incantation. Across the tracks, from her window, she continues to watch and tries to conjure their thoughts and words, ignoring for a while her unfinished draft. That train speeds off, carrying these mortals to another day through the hive and above, and its Babel of promises and power. She and her companions—with their stillborn promise, and muted lives, head elsewhere.

Left in the shadow of the station, the doors of her car remain open, no audible announcement. *An unplanned track repair, another vagrant cast out of the train, perhaps. No rush.*

The nurse has dried her tears with her coat sleeves, and starts to sit upright. She smiles at her, and the benediction is returned. The old man has gone to sleep, and some of his fumes mercifully escape into the brutalist tunnel. She looks back out through the window. Aided by the cabin lights and the dimness outside, she notices herself for the first time in months. She unfurls her hair, setting the beanie on the next seat. The strands are brittle and sparse; even in the dim reflection she can see through to her scalp. She begins to trace her cheekbones, pressing against threadbare ridges of skin. She lets out a sigh; her voice, once *full of money,* is now a faint rasp.

The last time she was this lucid was almost two years ago. Alone in the dusk and a flowerless room, she quietly reached for, unhinged, then dropped the IV bag on the linoleum floor. As she peeled the bandages, her eyes traced the crimson flowing out of her and into the tube, like an umbilical cord to another life. There, as the last of her companions and insurance dwindled, and before the orderlies rushed in shouting,

Eulogist

she imagined her father's last moments and the many she missed in the throes of her *Stateside* dream.

She shakes her head. As she tries to escape these images, she looks down at the damp floor; then, at her ankles, pale and mocked with veins. She starts to think about her mother. The one she never really knew, who now doesn't recognize her at all. Even if she scrabbled enough to fly homeward, after all these years, it wouldn't matter. Across meridians, and into an archipelago where the myths and memories mattered, there was nothing more to be roused from her. After her remittances had dried up, her sister's emails came fewer and farther between. They read like health bulletins that barely disguised resentment:

Mother's kidneys are failing. *Una, 'yung* neurologists, *ngayon* the encrin-ologists. *Malala na siya,...*

Her lips are blue, nothing comes out of them but screams. *Ate, wala na akong magagawa.*

ꓶꓶ

She's stopped eating na. Diyos ko, .

ꓶꓶ

Heto na. It should be a matter of days
Send what you can, *utang na loob!*

ꓶꓶ

Ate(h), malapit na and there's nothing to come back for.

White Flint. Twin Brook. Rockville.

I MUST FINISH THIS.

She types in the last few lines as the train emerges into the light. She looks at the last map she downloaded and saved, minimizes it, goes back to the draft, and whispers it one last time.

> *The good ferments*
> *the bad withers*
> *and trickles to completion.*
> *When you lose the words*
> *just listen for the mermaids' voice*
> *like the songs you once*
> *breathed in my ear...*
>
> *...you'll be closer*
> *to the constellations*
> *traced by your fingers*
> *The same ones that* abuelita
> *touched earlier.*
> *The ones that help you*
> *trace your journey home.*

As she scrolls down her screen to find her sister's email address, she is held back at the view before her as the train fords the river. Far from the monuments and marble, sprawled before her, lay the carcass of Western industry. The detail of rustbelts and strip malls emerge from the horizon, the same scenes that scattered the immigrants' ideals once they have crossed into the heartland, those *dark fields of the Republic*. And yet just footsteps away, she is not alone. Shorn of her past, there is someone farther still, waiting for her to arrive.

She waits for a feeble 3G bar to rise. There is an exclamation point on the battery icon. The file attaches. The tribute, hanging perilously on thin aether, is sent. *I know they will never read it to her. But she will know I said it.*

She sees an email from N. A long-winded apology. Desperately contrite, with a promise to finally take good care of her, to meet as soon as he flew back from assignment, to show her something. There is a trace of silent laughter, but all she notices are the hollowed eyes that stare back at her through the dimmed backlit panel.

...Shady Grove.

THE TRAIN ROLLS further, then halts. She is now on the other side. The driver's voice, loud with relief, calls out the last stop, ushering everyone off. She feels strangely awake: almost as if an appetite had started to return.

The card enters the slot, never again to emerge. She pushes past the turnstiles, not unlike the way she moved through the old playgrounds at Malate. Snow starts to fall as she crosses into Veirs Mill Road, and into St. Mary's. At the corner, from a newly minted billboard, Dr. Phi—tonsure, teeth, and time slot—looks onto the ashen landscape.

The hilltop, now powdered among the stones, starts to resemble a dream, or an opening chapter she can't place. *She beats on,* the ground damp with buried leaves and echoed footsteps.

She finds Him.

The last time she felt this way, she was at her grandfather's at Paco Memorial, in a now-forsaken part of Manila, a castoff within the city's ancient quarter. A stone's throw from her ancestral home, now rotting to its foundations. During her teens, before her father's petition came through, her aunts and the other family matrons had conspired to marry her off to a feeble, landed cousin. If that plan to restore the family fortunes didn't materialize, there was always the guaranteed grace of the convent to siphon off another ingrate.

Her father had read all her earlier stories and heartaches by her bedside. That never stopped, even as the words came through packets, in between stocking mess halls at the Navy's carriers. He would have none of that, and offered a way out. During those *Catolico-cerrado* days, where her mother helplessly stood by, she would storm off several streets away until all roads led to the moss-laden rotunda that once housed the martyr's memorial. There, she would find and stay with *abuelo*, who Papa said chronicled the Spanish, then American occupation as Homer did the Greeks. She would trace the etchings of writings on the tombstones with her eyes closed, and recite them as prayer. Before the sun set and the park closed, hold vigil at Rizal's emptied grave. There, prostrate on the ground of the martyred hero, she recited his words, making them her own. To both she swore to write of her nation, and then to never look back.

THIS MORNING, AS the faint sun reaches the headstones, she kneels, as she did then to another personal saint. She lays down his book. Her ungloved fingers have recited the lines, etched onto frozen stone.

She closes her eyes—as her arms raise, then smash the tablet where the slab meets Zelda's markings. She looks about her, will undiminished, even as she pats the snow for fragments. With all her reserves, she lifts the lifeless gadget once more—higher this time, and casts it down the unhinged corner of granite.

She lays her coat on the ground, and breathes in deep as she picks up a shard of the scattered display. It breaches the scar tissue, bringing her *ceaselessly* into the past.

Woke: A Love Story in Ambahan

THE LANAI WAS so muggy
that it almost slowed down those
darn mosquitoes still circling
around us, and I paused the
last dog rescue video.
It was a year of pigtails
and promises, I thought then,

drifting off until she said:
'Rub your eyes to see the stars,'
I placed my palm on her damp

forehead, careful not to disturb her
cowlicks and the IV lines
that stretched downward and across
the cool speckled marble floor,

into a pole and bag
of fluids and gravity that
would give her a chance at life.
Prying my hand from beneath
her arms, I did just that, and
swam in the patterns of light
and the dusk that unfurled like

starlings in the summer sky,
when I last saw *abuelita*:
stern, her hand clutching mine; the
other wiping my limbs
with *panyo de cara* to ease
the scarlet fever I caught
after wandering in the woods.

'Papa, tell me a story?'
And I drifted off, eyes closed,
whispering about the time
I followed this girl to shore,
and how she was really a
Tausug princess who saved
this feckless lad from drowning,

and hid him from her Father
because he came on a ship
of soldiers, stragglers, and priests
who destroyed everything they touched
and poisoned their people's blood.

That didn't stop His daughter
from visiting the fair boy,
caring for the stowaway,
bringing him water and yam,
and songs in their hiding place
in the forest, until he
suddenly fell ill; and she,
helpless and in tears, had no
choice but to tell the Datu.

Her Father relented, but
on the condition she knew
well ahead, as the warmth of
her embrace would not heal him.
The Imam came, summoned her
Ancestors who looked upon
the lifeless boy and saved him.

As the warriors escorted
him to the dark forest's edge
and to his waiting masters,
he looked back and into her
swollen eyes, and swore with his,
and all his returning strength:
I will see you again, love.

The light woke me up; I looked
down at the sleeping child with
tears drying on her flushed cheeks;
and as I stretched carefully,
I saw her mother smiling
at me from the glass picture frame.
Amina said, 'Find her.'

Woke: A Love Story in Ambahan

June 2020

Valparaiso

*"You know how when you're listening to music playing from another
room? And you're singing along because it's a tune you really love?
When a door closes or a train passes [and] you can't hear the music
anymore, but you sing along anyway... then, no matter how much time
passes, when you hear the music again, you're still in the exact time
with it. That's what it's like."*
—from *Music from Another Room*

GINA SET HER BASKET down as she ended her day off. She
unzipped her pink windbreaker and reached into her scrub
pocket for the last, few, remaining pesos to make her way
home. The steep, trolley ride all but separated her from that
last house on the hilltop. A long, spiral road lay before her,
one that resembled the first strands of life.

She sighed as the pre-war *ascensor* was closed yet again. Gina still had a fresh spring in her step from her last meeting, and decided to take the more laborious route after getting off the first tram on *Caleta Portales*. Her feet began to trace the circuitous path around the hill to her *amo*, whom she last left in a state of agitated torpor in the hands of her visiting daughter.

Santiago, her first port of entry, was in the throes of the pandemic. The headlines at the lonely paper stand and in her Twitter feed showed infections nearing the 300,000 mark: the highest count among the distant cities of this almost forgotten and underpopulated nation. One that she felt was hers to weave herself into, with a few, shared strands from her own.

Gina thought to herself how, just over a hundred miles from the capital, she was spared from the crossfire of the pandemic's reach. With Valparaíso harbouring just a tenth of the cases, she counted as her continued luck that her path led her away from the front lines and into the home of her patron, patient, and friend.

Tonight would be special, Gina thought, as she walked up the last stone steps, painted into a mural to look like piano keys. Dangling from her strained arm was the bag of crustaceans, condiments, and spices from the *Mercado El Cardonal*. There where she met with her fellow Overseas Filipino Workers who gave her the contraband at the bottom of the knapsack: a few dark, unmarked bottles of THC oil in crumpled brown paper for her unpredictable ward, enough to last the month until they saw each other again.

Gina sang wistfully through her N95 mask, then stopped. She looked around and removed it as the climb got steeper and her breaths grew more laboured. She stopped at the street landing separating the last flight before Collado Street, and sighed at the vista: the graffitied walls and uneven streets filled with garbage faded below her. Suddenly, the air warmed and lay stale. She resisted the desire to take another selfie and just paused to catch her breath—letting the moment, the new feelings of the day, take hold.

Looking below, Gina thought of how, in some ways, this port city resembled her southern hometown of Zamboanga. Its colonial buildings tracing the sea giving way to ramshackle structures past the sweep of the seafront. Up here, with the erstwhile crisp air and the promontories that stretched higher than any building back home, she could forget her cares. At this spot, everything below—from the sparse crowds to the noise of the remaining buses and cars—shrank in to blurred, faint miniatures and echoes.

She knew, from experience both at home and her two years here, that tonight would be different. With the motionless air and the gathering clouds far on the horizon, she sensed a storm approaching. This would be the first of the *temporales*, she thought. Or worse, *marejadas* that battered the coast months before the summer set in and with it, the Christmas holidays. That in itself made the season more familiar. Something Gina could wait for since the pandemic made her return home all but impossible. Chile's inverse, warmer weather by December, the Spanish greetings she could also bandy about with her *Chavacano* dialect in hand, helped anesthetize the longing for home. Even with the pandemic's threat of fewer, if virtual Masses and *Noche Buena* gatherings of a more terse and lukewarm people, she felt that it would be just enough to look forward to.

Gina gathered herself as she rushed up the final steps to the house. The last cross-street was now bathed in a faint golden hour, and she grew excited with her plan to treat her employer to a fancy, home recipe. She reached the faded red door at the end of the cul-de-sac, and reached for the brass knocker shaped like a woman's hand.

The door flung open.

"*¿¿Dónde te habías metido y qué andabas haciendo?!*" Gabriela looked through her.

"I'm sorry, I had to walk the rest of the way," Gina replied, trying to speak in cobbled, muffled Spanish through her mask to appease her, thinking she got home on time, if barely.

Gabriela trotted out her best English and it sounds even more offensive. "Can't you see I'll be late for my dinner in Santiago? You fucking Filipinos are all the same. And I bet you even took off that mask in the city. You're going to get us all sick and killed!"

"Ma'am, I was..."

"*No tengo tiempo para tus explicaciones!*" I expect you to clean up the whole day tomorrow and make up for your laziness— make sure I don't find a speck of dust in the upstairs bedroom when I come back next month, or get ready for a pay cut!" Gabriela's projected her high-pitched voice into the street. She swung her satchel around her shoulders and ran to the car across the street without looking back.

Gina turned around and shook her head, cursing under her breath. She started to worry about her own child growing up to be like that without her, when she heard the sonorous voice from across the hall.

"Never mind her. Am glad she's left us. Welcome back, *mi otra hija!*"

Gina moved through the hallway, walking ever so slowly, never failing to gaze at the provenance along the stucco walls. Here were monochrome photos from a bygone era: her patron under the spotlight showered with garlands at the *Teatro Municipal*, tours of the North American music halls and in the arms of *gringos*, a few framed images of smoke-filled supper clubs somewhere in Europe, toasts at banquets during the brief halcyon days with Allende, and somewhere in the centre of the curation, before the cavernous *sala*, that photo with Neruda, whom she proudly called "*mi Capitán.*"

The voice with the garbled accent at the end of hallway was Señora Carmen, the grand old dame of the house. She sat in her generous oak armchair, waving her brass bell as if to usher in a better, grander mood as she liked to do on days like these.

There's a storm coming *po...*" Gina liked to mix her native pleasantries with her responses, trusting her host to know what she truly meant in whatever tongue she spoke. Señora Carmen indeed fancied herself as a polyglot, a self-proclaimed world traveller at the height of her career.

"I know, *pobrecita*, and am glad you came just in time. It's coming, this storm: I can smell it in the air." Señora Carmen smiled.

One of the benefits of not having COVID, Gina chuckled to herself, as she walked over to the kitchen and set down the ingredients for tonight's meal. She was so pleased to have sourced all of these from her *suki* at the markets that plied the best of the Continent: chilies and turmeric from Mexico, curry powder from the Caribbean, coconut milk from Suriname, and today's fresh catch from the Chilean coast.

"*M'hija*, are you ready for your Spanish lessons after dinner to vanquish your pidgin dialect? Afterward, you can copy my photographs to that Instagram like you do your whole life." This was their weekly routine and barter, a way to pass the time and let the pictures prompt them to reveal the stories of their lives, a *palacio de memoria*, Señora Carmen liked to tease.

"Not tonight, *Tia Mameng*," Gina was feeling an extra sense of melancholy as she brought out the candles for the dinner table, even as she teased Señora Carmen with her local endearment, one she would only use when Gabriela or other guests were not around. "I thought I could share something new in my life, we need more time for this—even once the rains come, and we could continue even if the power goes out."

"Did I tell you about the time my Pablo was trapped, hiding in this house after the War, those days of the *Ley Maldita*..." The lilt in Gina's voice triggered something in her patient, with the siren song of memory tugging at her, and the mood lightened.

Only for the hundred seventeenth time, she sighed to herself, smiling at Señora Carmen, letting her continue as she turned up the heat underneath the pot that would boil their crawfish. It was a poor substitute for *curacha*—those densely beautiful coconut crabs. But no one would be the wiser, especially with the *aligui* sauce she would lavish on tonight's meal. It was one of those signature dishes she learned to make back home with her *abuelita* who was once the head cook at Alavar. Something she perfected with the other fare as she learned to feed her daughter by herself. A repertoire that flourished up until the board results came in and her overseas placement was secured.

With the lean crawfish turning bright red, Gina lowered the heat and returned to the story. Señora Carmen was at that point of the story where she reminisced about dropping everything in her life to follow her lover. She sailed alone with nothing more than a trunk of clothes, a purse full of jewellery, and a wellspring of love. All to have a rendezvous with Neruda while he was on exile. Her voice agitated as she recalled how she supported both of them by hustling for gigs at the jazz clubs, after the haughty opera houses had turned her down for just being barely *mestiza*. How there, in the din of the left-overs, cigarettes, unwanted advances and sleepless nights, she had lost her nerve. She said she felt, in between all that, ever the exile and pariah. And as she sighed, Señora looked fondly at Gina from afar, who was seemingly entranced by her shop-worn tale.

At that point in her life, she noticed how her curves, spunk, and desire for life had waned. Shortly thereafter, so did her Captain's ardour as he moved on with his insatiable, unforgiving appetites and pursuits. "The rest is history—the world's, and mine," Señora Carmen liked to say, as she shook her head back into the present as her corpulent body seemed to shrink from the retelling. Then she grew silent once more, looking out the window into the empty street below.

Gina nodded back, fatigue creeping in as thoughts turned to her child back home, now with her own *abuelita* and absentee husband taking more than his share of the remittances. Money that was spent, no doubt, on cockfights and mistresses and God knows what else. She planned to give herself extra drops of that magical-realist oil from Jaime. She planned to have a healthy dose after serving it with the *churros con chocolate* to her *Tia Mameng*, whose appetite had returned after a long bout of recovery.

So far, she still felt lucky: her patient hadn't had an episode since the operation to remove over a foot of her lower intestine a year ago. And it was certainly better than serving at the ER or a COVID wing of the *Servicio de Salud*, just half an hour's commute below, where she was originally assigned until the Gonzálezes intervened with the agency on behalf of their matriarch. Short enough of a distance to call for an ambulance there if Señora Carmen's bowels wouldn't cooperate, her cancer would suddenly return, or an accident would occur with her burgeoning weight and weaker limbs.

Tonight, the gales from below howled stronger and now reached the awnings of the old house. Large, piercing droplets of rain began to fall on the roof shingles of the house. But Gina knew they were safe and would celebrate to health and the good life that remained.

The dinner was uneventful and pleasant enough, with Gina thankful for the consolation of not having to make too much of a mess with the crustaceans as opposed to the unwieldy, complex anatomy of Pinoy coconut crabs. She and *Tia Mameng* devoured every morsel of flesh, rice, and sauce on her dainty, now splattered ceramic plates, all with the help of copious amounts of local Semillón from the *Alto Maipo.*

Señora Carmen was splayed out on her wooden throne, overwhelmed by the food, her mottled skin flush with grape. Gina would soon get her ready for bed, and as she looked outside at the drenched, darkening streets while rinsing the dinnerware, she felt a sudden lilt. With all the exhaustion, and shorn of all the filters and barriers she wore outside, a strange but familiar sense of desire remained. And with tonight's generous helping of wine, she was determined to tell her patron all about it.

"*Tia Mameng*, do you know Jaime, who gives us those magic potion drops? Well, he just told me he was leaving his wife and wanted to be with me... Me!" Gina sighed.

"Be careful, *m'hijita*, we have been down that mirage, that lonely road, too many times." Her patron's voice suddenly changed: it was almost as if the room grew darker even as the storm announced its arrival.

"But *Tia*..."

Señora Carmen suddenly cut her off, looking out the window across the table: "I thought he loved me, but he just needed me to survive. I could still recite all those poems by heart. The ones meant for me were easy to remember, but they left me empty, they were carelessly written, unpublished, all afterthoughts. I know it wasn't meant to last, *claro*, but I went along for the ride because I wanted to feel needed, even for a little while..."

"But this one, I remember...*escucha m'hijita:* my favourite poem, listen to this!"

Gina tried to translate with her head, but it was her heart that listened:

No, perdóname.
(Forgive me)
Si tú no vives,
(If you are not living)
si tú, querida, amor mío,
(if you, dear, my love)
si tú te has muerto,
(if you have died)
todas las hojas caerán en mi pecho,
(all the leaves will fall on my breast)
lloverá sobre mi alma, noche y día,
(it will rain on my soul, night and day)...

She tried to look up to remember how it ends, to try to stem the tears.

...mis pies querrán marchar hacia
(my feet will want to march to where you are sleeping)
donde tú duermes, pero seguiré vivo...
(but I shall go on living...)

"It still haunts me, this lack, this hollowed life... I am going to die soon and never be that woman..." Señora Carmen began to pound her fists on the table and started screaming.

Gina tried to assuage the old woman's rising anger. *"Tia Mameng,* but it was only a fantasy." She bit her lip, ruing those words, hoping they weren't understood. Before clarifying it was meant for the poem and not their love, Señora Carmen shouted back: "And he had the gall to come back here, buy that crooked house across my hilltop, and pretend I never existed, not even when he left her for good!"

Nag-juramentado na naman si Ma'am, Gina thought to herself as she consoled her *Tia Mameng* and then lifted her off her throne and slowly helped her walk to her makeshift bedroom across the dining area.

"I want to see *La Sebastiana* from up there and shout to his ghost. Ven, bring me to the upstairs balcony so I can tell him he ruined me for anyone else!" Señora Carmen almost knocked Gina down with her speckled forearms as she screamed and flailed away in rage.

Gina composed herself for a moment and they walked again. This time, not into the bedroom, but towards and up the stairs, carefully, two pairs of footsteps at a time, heaving with all her might until she all but gave up after reaching the cold, bare landing of the stairway.

It was too dangerous for her to leave Señora Carmen alone in the middle of the flight while fetching the cannabis oil. She had to gut it out by embracing her with all her might, hoping the *temporal*, and with it, *Tia Mameng*'s tempest, would pass.

"Ma'am *calma lang*, please *po—A ver, tranquila...por favor no se enoje*, please *Tia Mameng, maawa na po kayo...*" Gina pleaded as she held Doña Carmen's wrist, decorated with liver spots and scars. She was careful not to let her other hand lose control and let the colostomy bag fall and spill its contents down the varnished steps.

"*Subamos, m'hija*, please, my dear, just this once. Please." She broke down, crying into Gina's bruised shoulder, and soon, Gina let her tears fall, too, as the dead weight of the old woman's body eased onto her frame, her back on the balustrade.

The winds howled for what seemed like a long time. In those hours, and the delta between the sill and glass, a few droplets of the settling rain reached their forehead and shoulders. It cooled the humid languor of the house, and the searing rage within.

They held each other tightly until the percussion of the rain slowed its tempo. Then the wind stopped howling, leaving something else to whisper through the window opening.

After what seemed to be hours and having fallen asleep, it was Señora Carmen who woke up her guardian:

"*Mira hacia arriba, m'hijita!* Look up!"

"*¡Ay, escuche Señora Carmen!*—Gina, fully alert now, responded.

In the growing silence between the falling of the raindrops, the music had found its way to them. A woman across the street had opened her windows. She began to welcome the dawn with a song, in this language Gina barely shared, but whose chords they both knew by heart. One who once sang this in her prime; the other who knew this, hummed to her and sung by her as a lullaby.

The voice grew stronger as the rains ceased, as if to heed that longing through the windows that separated them from each other and the outside world. It scaled the walls that barely concealed desire, now emerging from another isolated, opened room with this anthem. It travelled through the cleansed air, through meridians of this dormant hemisphere, and plumbed the recesses of memory. They began to look up, smiling as they closed their eyes to trace this hymn:

> ...*Que una paloma triste*
> *(a sad dove)*
> *muy de mañana le va a cantar,*
> *(early in the morning will sing)*
> *a la casita sola*
> *(at the lonely house)*
> *con sus puertitas de par en par.*
> *(whose small doors are widely open)*
> *Juran que esa paloma*

(They swear that his dove)
no es otra cosa más que su alma,
(is none other than his soul)
que todavía la espera
(that is still waiting)
a que regrese la desdichada.
(for the unhappy woman to return)
Cucurrucucú paloma,
(Oh dove)
cucurrucucú no llores.
(don't cry)
Las piedras jamás, paloma,
(the stones we walk on, dove)
¿qué van a saber de amores?
(will never know of love)
Cucurrucucú, cucurrucucú,
cucurrucucú, paloma, no llores
(cry no more, dove)

Mercury Rising

"BABE, MY BATTERY'S DYING," he says, as the bride and groom finish their dinner and stand up.

"I told you to stop posting nonsense on FB. No one cares about your feed!" Lani frowns.

"You didn't even take the right angles of me *kanina* —such a useless IG boyfriend you are!"

"Uhmmm, my speech is coming up and I won't have enough juice to read my notes," he says, sheepishly, looking down—slightly away from the phone, but just enough to check the latest Lego demo video.

Left of the presidential table, Lani's girdled corpulence spills over just enough to snap a few selfies of herself, the cake, and the lovely couple making their way to the stage.

"Get me a G&T—nothing lower than Tanqueray, and make sure the tonic's sugar-free—the pink one, yeah?" she waves him off and as he looks back, she starts uploading a storm herself.

He chats up the bartender with some relief from his soon-to-be fiancée, then turns to the band leader who compliments his Wolverine cuff links while they go over the set, milking the interlude as long as he can while the program drones on.

He returns with two glasses in hand, smiling as the ballroom lights go dim. "Here you go, babe: they actually had the No. 10, so we're covered."

"By the way, you look so beautiful tonight, my darling." Looking at her, he believes every word he said as his eyes trace upwards, from swollen gown to face. Those fierce, lovely cheekbones buried by jowls that bore a fair share of entrees all these years—now growing redder than the rouge she had slathered all morning.

"Where's dessert? Don't you know I need to have my cocktails with something for my ulcer!? And is that why you took so long? I bet you downed some cupcakes—God, look at your gut: it's so gross! You're not taking care of yourself—or me!!!"

She shakes her head as she grabs the nearest glass, nearly spilling all of it on his *barong* sleeve.

"Give me your glass: you need to drive *pa* later—and you get super soft after a few of those." She chugs it in one go, her gargling sounds muffled by the bridesmaid's bawling tribute.

He looks away from his hangry queen and takes a deep breath. This is the year, he thinks. *Make or break.* Turning 35, and with Pops kicking the bucket not far from his age, he wanted this to be an inflection point. Marriage, babies, the bungalow, the whole smorgasbord on his shoulders. She was trudging near 40, and insisted she wanted that, too, so this was it. No turning back. Never mind if she almost mauled him during the last quarrel when he didn't back down over something that he couldn't fathom, let alone remember. He couldn't even recall if she said sorry, *but she's been so sweet me since*, he tells himself.

He sits quietly as the chatter grew in the ballroom. Then he fishes for his phone from his pleated trousers, and panics at the red sliver on the battery icon. The host starts eyeballing him from the stage to let him know he's next.

"Babe, can I send my notes and the lyrics to your messenger so I can use yours instead? Promise I won't pry and will give it back after I'm done—I'm up next."

Lani rolls her false-lashed eyes, punches in a few commands, then hands it over like a Dowager dispenses *ang-pau*.

He comes up the stage, stays on the side before the last parents wind down their benediction, and downloads his script.

He clicks on it, starts to memorize the bullets, and scrolls down to recite the lyrics he already knows by heart, but lip-synchs just the same from nerves. He winks at the band across and gives them a thumbs up.

Lani is staring at him, watching both his eyes and fingers on the screen; and after a few seconds, starts whispering to her *amigas* in the table, leaving him alone on the darkened side stage.

"Hello everyone, my name is Rico, uhmm, the best man..."

The spotlight is now on him, and he tries to look into the audience, by now restless, but drowned out by the glare. He squints at the backlit screen and his notes, which he can barely see through the lights and nerves.

"Try as I might, I'm at a loss for words...so to paraphrase one of my favourite films, if you want to be completely honest, just sing."

"This one's for you, lovebirds..." They look at him in earnest, tinged with pity and trepidation, then each other, into their cocktails, but not before each giving Lani a passing, toothless glance.

He starts off with the words he knows, then points to the band; and, the show is on.

> *"This thing, called Love..."* [His voice cracks...]
> *...I can't handle it*
> *This thing, called Love, I must get around to it*
> *I ain't ready, crazy little thing called Love..."*

That's all he can wing. He tries to sway as he strains to look at the lyrics, then feels the vibration from the phone.
Messenger bubble pops up.

> Günter: *"Porkpie—can't wait 'til you get back..."*

He clicks on it, scrolls up, doesn't see the thread.
Ellipses... new bubbles.

> Günter: *"Spread your thighs and take snaps your flower for me when you can— I'll feed it good and make you scream more than your geek-boy."*

> Günter: *"Afternoon delight Monday?"*

The glare and gin numb the gut punch he feels at the centre of his body. The lyrics are seething through his teeth while his swollen thumbs fiddle a response.

> Lani: *"Just you wait..."*

He/she presses send—then points to the bandleader for the coda, and goes back to the lyrics. Shaking his head during the instrumental, he starts remembering the "girls' nights out" binges in Poblacion and God-knows-where that got more frequent over the last few months. And, how the wanker actually made an appearance at least once—and even had the nerve to join them during Valentines' Quiz Night. Jeezus, he thinks. *He even finished my drink—then walked off,* after whispering in her multi-pierced ear.

He now recognizes that same grin on her face all those times she stopped to text or leave the room to take her "boss's" calls.

He looks up:

> *"There goes my baby*
> *She knows how to rock and roll*
> *She drives me crazy*
> *She gives me hot and cold fever*
> *Then leaves me in a cool, cool sweat..."*

The band starts riffing; he loosens the top mother-of-pearl button, and starts strutting with abandon. He locks eyes with Lani with reflexive schadenfreude; she stares back with those smoky eyeshadows in mock ardour and curdling disgust.

Rico takes one last look at her trusty OPPO Selfie Pro3. The ballroom comes alive and starts singing along.

> *"I gotta be cool, relax, get hip*
> *and get on my tracks*
> *Take a back seat, hitch hike,*
> *And take a long ride on my motorbike*
> *Until I'm ready – Freddie!!!* [he screams]
> *Crazy little thing called love."*

With that jolt of umbrage and liberation, he starts to remember the discography, and drops the smoking gun of a gadget to the stage like it was both a Mercury prop and Pandora's box—stomps it like a stoned, jilted Brian May, and turns his back on the crowd until they go nearly silent.

He doesn't see Lani, but knows her eyes are now fixed on him, and in that moment they both were finally on the same, unfiltered plane.

His legs start shimmying, almost involuntarily, as the band ramps up for the final refrain.

He pivots, looks to the band and motions them to cut the music.

Rico now swings full frontal to the audience, projecting his solo voice with a guttural hum. He channels the dead frontman, he lets it all out before jumping from the stage, slicing through the muted hall, and into his car to finish the anthem and begin his life.

> *"I want to break free...*
> *God knows I want to break free..."*

February 2014

Eventide

I am the Sea,
cut and folded;
I am the last evening fallen
on an enchanted shoulder
—"What the Rose Said," Michael Hannon

THE WINDOW LET IN some of that magic hour I'd grown accustomed to.

"How was your day, my darling?"

My hand stretched across to caress hers. While she didn't shirk back, she didn't clasp it either.

"Five minutes early this time, love...and look at what I brought you!"

My hand coiled back to pull out the frame holding a collodion print of us: locked in an endless gaze; or at least long enough for the exposure to take hold.

"Remember when you taught me to trust and keep still — and let light, time, and molecules do their magic? I believe you. Take a look."

I took care not to leave fingerprints on the pane bordered with *narra* strips I had salvaged in her studio, dovetailed together each day I got home from work, hewed until it fit.

"Back then, love, we had all these plans. You said—*please look at me*—right at the click of that shutter, that whatever happens, we would take care of each other. Don't you remember?"

"Time will darken it." She discarded the portrait with her eyes, her hands retreating beneath the table's surface.

At that point I didn't know if she was talking about the image: how the emulsions on glass slowly congeal, spread, then fade over time in the presence of air, like a silenced womb. Or, maybe about what remained between the two of us.

She looked around the room, faintly lit by the candles I had arranged before coming up. Our shadows loomed on the nearest wall as she spoke.

"We look so different...I looked so different."

She did. We both did. And those eyes that once gazed at me—with me—*now looked through me.*

"Why did you bring me here?"

"But love, this is where..."

"I want to go home."

"But this..."

"Take me home. Now!" She scowls at me: her anger, visceral and blunt.

She looks down at her empty plate, almost as if to see her reflection, and at that point I don't know if she recognized what had just happened.

Right then and there I wanted to smash the glass plate on my knee, that projection of love and us. I took deep breaths, stood up, and shook my head: it was really all I had left of her, of us . I walked to the edge of the room and placed our photograph on the shelf that still harboured the scent of the bouquet I'd laid there last week.

From the corner, I looked past her, too, toward the surrounding dusk and that bird on the wire outside the steel window. It was the same, unremarkable one from before; almost always watching us—I swear it could have recited that same conversation by rote.

I approached, carefully, until I stood close enough to lean downward to try and place her head as close to my heart. She didn't resist, but her arms didn't reciprocate to meet mine, only to push ever so slightly, to glance at my face. I could barely look back, because of what I knew I wouldn't find each time I kept my gaze any second longer.

She said no more to me even as her lips were pursed and trembling. I pressed the buzzer, and as help came, she looked away and into the waiting nightfall.

There would be no stars tonight, not by the open parking lot I'd pace around aimlessly, bracing myself before each visit, asking for some sign.

I stepped out into the hallway where the gurneys and orderlies stood motionless, speechless. I shut the door behind me, not looking back. The noise of my heels, dragging on the linoleum, ceased when I stopped to look at the muted TV on the wall. There I stayed, long enough to finish that lingering scene of a *Mission Impossible* sequel we'd glossed over in a crowded cinema long ago—the one where Ethan Hunt sprints and leaps off, tethered to the side of a round, desert skyscraper, only to miss the opening from a shattered glass wall.

That was the last time she held me close, and truly looked at me, amid the darkness.

And this shard in my stomach is replaced with the void of falling.

November 2028

Homecoming

OVER THE LAST DECADE, he'd spent his birthdays in transit. By himself. On his own terms.

This year was no different. At least that's what he tells himself as he flips the master switch, latches the fuse box, and pats his pockets. He looks at the frozen river through the curtain gap, and double-bolts the door. He detects a whiff of java, ever a tad weak compared to what he grew up with. There are a few dregs in the cup he can still put to work. *Never mind. You're cutting it too close this time.* The Virgin Tesla shuttle sends a notification through his timepiece. He heads down the stairwell, out the door, and like many of his journeys, does not bother to look back.

He is going home; rather, to the place he was born.

It is a long way from Reading, and a jarring ride to get to Gatwick. He hardly smiles at the courtesies that get him through the lanes as he waves his golden badge and its vaccine QR strip, and tattooed blue passport. He breezes past the lounge this time, reaching the farthest gate but not before cursing British infrastructure for the nth time. *It's 2028, not the bloody Thatcher era!*

Upon entering the cabin, he is ushered leftward to his seat, and settles into his routine. The pills, downed with bourbon, have unshackled meridians and disemboweled time.

Another long hauler: this time, eastward. Enough shut eye to catch up from the number-crunching numbness and caffeine drips of the last quarter. *The Westward routes are harder,* he tries to convince himself, but this time he feels slightly heavy, if not unhinged. The eyelids begin to falter and drop, but not before a glance at an exquisite set of cheekbones. Hoisted onto them are wire-rims, hiding darkened eyes panning through a dog-eared journal. Her ringless fingers adding cursive Italian to the margins. He makes out the word *tribù,* and tries to decipher the rest. She smiles as she catches him. His face is flushed, from this and the cocktail. Feigning impatience, he raises his hand, thinks of calling for a refill. He tries to fight it but can't.

THEY ARRIVE, earlier than expected. In his stupor, fumbling for his briefcase and rushing to the gates, he forgets to introduce himself.

Thought we had enough time, he rued. *No more spiking liquid courage...There will be others.*

She has gone ahead, past the cold granite corridors of Chep Lak Kok. Their queues are parted, but not before seeing her, glancing back at him. There is that dusk in her eyes, almost wanting to say something before it's too late. He looks down, fumbles for his phone. The spell is broken.

He is at his gate, heading to another world. Hesitation prevailed yet again, and in its wake, the questions. Why the beads in her necklace were unnervingly familiar. Almost like the colour of the betelnut stain on his forefathers' teeth. Will she return East, and when? He was from a nation, if you could define his people as such, of barely a quarter million. He is making his way back to a country of castes and a hundred thirty million more blokes, and all he cared about was whether he would find her, amidst all that flawed humanity. It didn't matter right now; he had reached the commuter connection to Laoag International just in time, and soon would be signing up for a rental.

He paid his penance by stepping harder on the accelerator, thinking the car could outrun his memories. Through the rain-blurred windshield, the mountains of his boyhood loomed larger on his right, bidding him to draw nearer.

He could barely keep to the right side of the road with the downpour lulling him into thinking he was back on the A1. As he shook his head from his stupor, the almost-forgotten landscapes announced themselves to him. To his left, as he sped down the husk strewn roads lay the coastline that seemed almost frozen in time. To his right, the mountains and their lurking myths.

The last book he had read travelling the other way, decades back, was Tolkien's. He thought to himself: *Isn't it curious that Middle Earth could very well be the Cordilleras?* There were the dwarves and their mines, and they very well could have been the *Itnegs* and the *Yapayaos*, their crimson mountains reminding him of Erebor. The dark-skinned, ornately adorned *Gaddangs*, short in stature but statuesque in lore and hospitality, almost like hobbits. Then there were the *Kankana-eys*, the "chosen ones", civilised by the Anglicans.

Their rise contrasted with his own tribe, the *i-Kalinga*, whom the rest of the world would brand as savage head hunters. *That makes us the fucking orcs*, he squirms, as he drives through tortuous roads into Cagayan valley, the last threshold before his hinterland. His only consolation is that these scattered, strange peoples and bedfellows all live far enough away from the poison of the colonisers, the decadence of the lowlanders, and the rest of the riff-raff that stifled the rest of the mainland.

The vehicle had traced the stubborn ridges of Northern Luzon, and now makes its way down the nape of the main island. Memories undulate as the rice terraces come into to view as memories intermingled.

IN ONE OF THE BODLEIAN exhibits a decade back, he chanced upon *Las Islas Filipinas*—the Galleon traders', then the Missionaries' archives on the natives. One of the panels showed a seminal map from the 1700s, used by the Governors-General as Hispanisation moved inward of Luzon and into the fabled mountain ranges. There in front of him stood a mural-sized slap to his people: the colonised tribes, all named and recognized: *Igorots, Ibalois, Bontocs, Ifugaos* and the rest...and then deep in the centre, like a black hole, a forbidding pubis, was his province, his people; the only heathens who refused. Their name, painted diagonally in bright red letters across the territory: LOS INFIELES.[1]

---

[1]   The Infidels.

THE ODOMETER REACHES 90 and he settles into cruise control. He rustles through the sheaf of papers. With the other hand on the wheel, he steadies his advance while committing his mind to those blueprints, his talking points, and to get out of there not a moment later. *You've put this off too long. Get it over with, and then you can go back to your life. And maybe, just maybe, find her.*

The road starts to wind again, this time upward. The forested hills give way to coarse grassland, a tawdry consolation salvaged by nature after logging concessions had their fill. He reaches the city plateau of Tabuk. Gone are the acacias that lined the wide, once dirt road, and in its place potholed cement and gaudy, smuggled streetlights have started to light up as dusk approached.

He drives past the capitol: a neo-classical rip-off painted in red and black stripes, the only tribute to his people's culture. He turns right past the monstrous Cathedral that was erected on a hill-mound that his forebears had considered sacred.

He crosses the rusty bridge, over the ancient rocks, stripped naked from the now-trickling Chico River, vanishing even more as the pick-up struggles upward on the trail. As the high beam meets the spreading carpet of fog, he feels that strange, empty feeling once more.

The sign toward his village lies unhinged and swaying on a gnarled post. He parks the car by the clearing. As he puts up the handbrake he feels his seat, the chassis, vibrating madly. He shakes his head and looks around him to steady himself: the mountain faces have been sheared to the marrow, and the gorges below are now naked, mineralized like herringbone. He walks out of the truck. A smell of rotten eggs grows stronger as he peers over the edge. The only thing that keeps him steady is the wind—howling, but emptied of its voice. The wind that once gently carried across the vibrant chants of warriors and their mates, stories and songs. The force he had spent his adult life to measure in Dover as he trained to harness its energy for a waiting world.

Several steps below, the trail leads to another one at the neck of the village. There is the local office of the National Commission on Indigenous Peoples. The outpost pales in comparison with the larger annex at an angle to the building, with a larger marquee, "Ibanag-Xiamen Resources Corp." The sound of quarrying trucks echoes from the valley below. Way before his pick-up, the rot from mainland China and the low-lands have already found its way to the villages.

He strays from the trail even as he looks up, and he sees the familiar firelight in the highest dwelling, beckoning him to come. His head is still swelling from the hangover, the scorched nostalgia, and the missed opportunity with another traveller. He decides against it.

I will announce myself, and only then visit Apo.

"LOOK WHO WE have here! Tell us your name." A man glowers while the entourage smiles in approval. His eyes are reddened with gin, clothes and accent Westernised into grue-some caricature.

"Victor Daguio," he steps forward, into the crowded office. "I'm here to meet with *Apo Lakay* and our Council of Elders." His voice rises as he smelt the gin and dried paint. "We're bringing renewable energy to this place, our people, and a whole new way of living that doesn't need all this, you, or your lousy yellow partners." As he says it, he starts feeling his occidental Oxbridge swagger trample the threshold.

"No, *obing*, your real name," the man sneers back.

Homecoming

He has never uttered it since he left.

"Say it!"

"...*Banna...*" he mutters, as he looks down.

"Aha—the 'noble warrior' returns! We were told you were coming. But your clan's time is over, and your kind's no longer welcome here. We now own your land, and your people...I bet your head's filled with all these clever ideas, but all we're doing is taking what's ours. Our Chinese cousins have been doing business here for centuries, and now they're with us. We've just made it official!"

The man points to the wall. He sees a map, speckled with mineshafts, and right at the centre, a monstrous grey casino complex at the heart of a new wasteland, with the Pasil River that ran below them blackened like the ink on the poster.

"Glad you could drop *here* first. Times have changed, boy. We're in charge now. Your Elders have dried up like the riverbed. No one here shows up for your *kanyaos* anymore. Do you even remember what they looked like? Come on, dance for us!"

The room starts to echo with howls. He shakes his head and grits his teeth amid the verbal onslaught, and can almost feel the walls tremble around him.

"So, *Balatoc*-boy...Show us your tattoos!" He looks down, and stays silent.

"Not even one? Hah! You are the last pathetic stalk of a dead people. They're all gone, like the mind of the old man. He's forgotten everything—his duties, his Gods, and yes, *you...*"

There is stomping and jeering, and some have begun to stand up and start to surround him.

"The mines are set for blasting; the licences have all been sewn up, thanks to our partners. We're gonna split first the ore down the middle before you get to grow balls...Then you can bring *your kind* to the card tables and watch your sisters dance at ours!"

He tries to stand taller, to get a word in. The man waves him off and kicks the chair.

He remembers how battles started amongst his ancestors, when causes were nobler, and the stakes were much clearer.

The door closes behind him. He can no longer hear the wind, but the sound of a gathering storm, and rain rapping through the lone window. He steels himself, summons enough to rise above this brewing tumult. He tries to speak, but nothing comes out. He tries to reach inside his bag for his papers, to prove his point. A clap of thunder floods the room. Within a sudden breath, his sight darkens as a searing shock radiates through his chest, like the moment before a wound proves blood.

HIS EYES OPEN to the sound of throttling engines. The smell of stale, pungent coffee is all around him, and mirth-fully accented apologies. He is on seat 32c, next to the woman who has taken him away from a dream, and into her world. He feels her napkinned hand flutter and dab around his caffeinated breast-pocket.

He looks out into the darkened, rain-riddled sky, but sees himself, back again in the communal throes of the dance— flames and songs mingling with the spirits of the elders and the next generation as a man and woman become one.

Behind them watches grandmother as she wipes *Apo Lakay's* brow, his sweat mingling with the saliva and betel nut stains on the ground, the very colour of the heirloom around her neck. They now look at him, and he sees them whispering to each other. He strains to understand.

Homecoming

The engines grow louder, but he can still hear the copper *gangsa* clanging with the footsteps pounding the ground. The pilot recites his spiel as wheels are unleashed to meet the tarmac. The *Ullalim* dance unfolds around them; the tyres touch the asphalt as the cabin lights drown everything else.

Returning his stanched landing card, and not before gleaning the scribbled dates, she smiles.

*"Auguri, caro...*We're here."

Hejira

*Dedicated to the memory and unfinished legacy of Kian, Emmanuel,
Myca, Kim, and their lengthening constellations in the night sky*

RICHIE STOOD BY the water's edge, and took off his mask at the foot of the crimson bridge marking the halfway point of their escape. The little Lumad girl was still asleep, cooled with the half-rolled down window, hidden in the blanket-lined recesses of the wagon he borrowed from Uncle Leon back in Davao.

As the brisk breeze receded with the warmth of the Eastern Visayan morning, he looked back one more time at the lapping waves and steadied himself for the gathering storm.

He entered the car, steeled himself for the checkpoint, and with the rolled down window said *'Maayong Buntag'* to the man holding the Armalite rifle and sweating through his face shield. Between his mental face palm and the Sergeant's response, it seemed like an eternity as the man looked inside and saw the child. *'Maupay nga adlaw, pasensya'*— *nag-ro-roadtrip kami papunta kay Lola sa Maynila,'* fumbling through his Arrneow accent. The soldier took one more look around and, as he faced the boot of the car, got startled when Gandalf, Richie's stowaway mongrel, stood up in half-growl. The officer stepped back and motioned for them to speed off as the phalanx of travellers piled up behind them.

ALL THINGS CONSIDERED, it had been an uneventful six-hour, non-stop drive from Tibungco to Surigao. The trip was filled with foliage and lakes he could barely make out from the plane that first took him on his journey to Mindanao several months back, with the pain on his arm from the newly minted vaccine keeping him awake on that early morning flight. Now reaching the sunset ferry, Richie welcomed a tinge of levity on the first leg of his drive. In contrast with the dread he'd felt picking her up with the hastily borrowed beat-up station wagon he christened Sandra Bulok in honour of his *Birdbox* heroine, not knowing how they would last the trip North.

Tita Bel, his homestay mother, woke him up earlier than his 5 a.m. start for English classes at his adopted village over three miles away. Tibungco was so congested and prone to more lockdowns with homes of teeming families, that he was forced to look for a dwelling place in the next settlement.

He began his 'gap' year bringing little else than a swollen tote bag filled with lived-in jeans, Uniqlo dri-fits, *tsinelas*, his gadgets, the JVP binder, the vaccine booster prescriptions.

This was a community he'd trained for and knew by briefs and reports from the volunteer before him, and gradually got to know with a reciprocated caution over his first few months of testing his newly-minted Bisaya and lesson plans.

All of that changed when shots rang past midnight. Richie thought these were the usual overripe mangoes dropping on the *yero* in his little *sitio*, or distant thunderclaps from the oncoming monsoon season that would mark the second half of his assignment. Maybe it might have been the usual *pasaway* liquor ban-curfew violator getting his due from Davao's finest. But as he began stirring from the screams of the usually unflappable Tita Bel, he then realized that things had changed for everyone.

FREED FROM THE checkpoint, the wagon slowly traversed the crimson marvel that was San Juanico Bridge. Richie breathed a sigh of awe and relief, disinfecting his hands while steadying the wheel. In the silence of the morning's arrival, a Led Zeppathon in his head, him humming along as they drove gently over cantilevered steel and water. The constancy of the bulletproof diesel engine rattling blended in with his senses embracing everything he had seen, and the mission he'd been placed into.

Soon, the verdant topography of Leyte and much of Mindanao, the azure sea in between would give way to a harsher, forbidding landscape. Into their Samar leg, the wagon's air-conditioning was no match for the garish sun as they made their way through parched, winding hills. Soon, the girl would wake up as Richie's newly-minted driving skills met the motley road's resistance. The novelty of this maiden, cross-country journey began to wear off. His last and longest road trip being the weekly Alabang—Loyola Heights carpool shift, and in an automatic SUV before the university and virus forced everyone off campus.

The wagon's body let out more frequent noises as it wound through the brown hillsides and scattered *kubos* and the occasional livestock. Gandalf, panting with the heat at the rear, jumped into the passenger seat and woke up the little girl, unstartled as she welcomed him into her arms, hugged him until they both settled back into the rhythms of Richie's driving, and fell asleep once more.

With the quiet resuming and arid landscapes darkened by the looming clouds, he looked once more for signs to the next port and its checkpoint. He knew he was close; his smartphone resumed vibrating, with pent up messages coming through as they fell within range of the cellular towers.

We're near the main town then, he thought, as he glanced at the crumpled national highway map he used in place of the Waze-less network coverage and worries of leaving a digital footprint.

After he stopped to pee against the hillside brush, before the city came into view, he unlocked his phone to scroll for messages. They were from the Programme Director in Manila.

NKQSJ: *Where are you?*
Me: *Sorry am OK, reached Samar, near port*
NKQSJ: *Calling you now*

The phone rang and he picked up right outside the car, ever mindful of the silent girl.

"Richie, will make this quick."

"O.K., Father."

"They know. No time to waste. The Provincial Superior's reached across the spectrum, a *Supernumerary* will meet you in Calbayog. You're familiar with them, no?"

"Wow, desperate times, Father Noli..." Richie liked to tease his liberal Loyola mentors for veering leftward and off the deep end, versus his parents' belated Opus Dei formation, with him waffling towards the middle.

"No time for jokes, kiddo." Fr. Noli's voice grew stern. "Listen. St. Peter and Paul Cathedral...third confessional to the right of the altar."

"Father, how much danger, how much time?"

"A couple of days, maybe three. Your Uncle Leon tells me that's just enough to get her into Manila, into our shuttered campus before we secure passage. I've had the Provincial speak to your folks, who know a thing or two of restraint, and the Ambassador. They all know what to do. Shut your phone and show up before sunset this Tuesday at the latest."

"Will bring her in safely, Father Noli." He could sense trepidation from his mentor's voice. After all, in this whole scheme of things, he wasn't the first choice for the original assignment. Richie barely made the cut for the Jesuit Volunteer program, which aimed to get the crème de la crème of his peers off into the boonies to fight for social justice upon graduation. He remembered how Fr. Noli had told him, after he finally received his acceptance letter, how he overruled the selection committee because he knew 'God would make a good example of you when the time came.' That private debt had now come due, and this memory seared inside him as the dropped call. The abrupt promise made him want to relieve himself again, after which he shut the car door, took a deep breath, and sped off into the town.

WHEN TITA BEL woke him up two days ago, Richie had been struggling with a dream he's had for months: it always starts with him fixing the knot on his Hermes necktie, a graduation gift from his girlfriend, while preening at the glass entrance of a skyscraper in a three-piece suit. He picks up his grandfather's briefcase, fixes his face shield to pry loose the cowlicks of his hair, and enters a high-speed elevator. As soon as Richie gets in, he's met by an elevator operator with shiny blue eyes, who proceeds to remove her mask as they speed upward. His breathing quickens as he recognizes the Virgin. Only each and every time it's a different version of her, like the ones he'd see in the different murals and grottos around the world.

That particular night, She was in plain clothes—distressed jeans and a button down—no less divine and unnerving. And as with all midpoints of the dream, there she would be, smiling: asking him where he'd like to go. In each instance he would rattle off a different destination, a different part of his life, past of future that he'd like to change or witness. Only this time, he stumbles; and for the first time, shrugs and says: "you choose, my Lady."

TITA BEL SLAPPED him on his exposed cheek, peeled him away from foetal position, and as soon as he opened his eyes, he thought he was back in another dream, wanting to wake up again. She told him *Manong* Ben had been shot dead in his house in the middle of the night, back in one of the shanties of Tibungco. The police had barricaded the tiny house, and one of the *usiseros* started screaming about planting drugs by the body. Rushing from next door to his aid, *Manong* Ben's sister too, was gunned down. That left Fatima, who had followed her to the scene, running from her dying mother, across the makeshift football pitch had Richie set up months ago, into the darkness and Imam Ali's arms.

"*Dong! Dong! Mata dong mata dayun!!*"
"*Ha? Ngano Tita? Unsay nahitabo!?*"

"*Gipatay si Aling Sorhaiya bag-o lang gyud! Gipusil siya sa mga pulis!*"

"*Bakit naman po Tita, anong kelangan nating gawin?*"

He couldn't translate the Bisaya quickly enough in his stupor.

"*Dong! Pagdali na! Pag-impake ug adto sa siyudad kay init pa diri!*"

Even with the light streaming into the homestay, they still heard police sirens wailing, almost nearing. Tita Bel and Richie stuffed what they could into his bag. As they made their way out of the house, Imam Ali was waiting outside in his tricycle, with the skinny nine-year old girl wrapped in a blanket in the sidecar. "*Assalamu Alaikum,*" he said to his friend and fellow football coach to the Lumad children of the village, as he squeezed in after hugging Tita Bel, promising her he would take care of the little girl. After they settled into the tricycle, Imam Ali sped to the main highway and into the outskirts of the compound of his Uncle Leon where Ali told them what had happened.

Uncle Leon, a true Mindanawon, U.S. *balikbayan*, whose genteel family belonged to the original settlers in Davao, wasted no time: he knew the drill. Knowing the President all too well, he hurriedly packed supplies into the wagon—a sleeping bag, bananas from the plantation, a jug of water, his daughter's old Adarna story books. And, for good measure, Gandalf: the Weimaraner-Aspin mixed mutt. Gandalf took to Richie every time he'd visited, and was up and about, circling the unannounced visitors, and now sniffing and licking the little girl's face. She seemed startled with a dog of a size she'd likely never seen, and looked like she wanted to scream, but didn't. It was then Imam Ali and Richie looked at each other and realized the trauma of the shootings had rendered her unable to speak at all.

As Imam Ali tucked her in the back seat, Gandalf jumped into the wagon's boot, and Uncle Leon locked the door, handed the keys to Richie. He whispered instructions in his ear, telling him he would make the arrangements with his embassy friends, and not to worry. He then gave him a hug that more than made up for over a year of withdrawn contact and protocols. Catching his breath after lifting Richie off the ground, he said thank you, and to Imam Ali: '*Shukran, Assalamu Alaikum.*'

'*Hafidaka Allah,* my friend, and our jewel's protector.' Ali embraced, shook his hand, and placed his palm on his heart. And with that, they were off and headed up North.

THE CALBAYOG HEAT was overwhelming, befitting its name, as the wagon teetered into the Cathedral's parking grounds. Gandalf jumped off the rear as soon as he lifted the door, and he gently lifted the girl, now crying from the dizziness, heat and hunger from the tortuous drive, with him trying in vain to help her put on a mask.

The Cathedral's main doors were closed, but they snaked around until they found the side entrance. There he asked Gandalf to stay outside and watch, and they both entered, passing the alcoves, and into the main chamber with its ornate whitewashed altar. He left the Lumad, Muslim girl by the first row, keeping his eyes side-glanced on her as he entered the confessional, with his heart racing again.

He heard breathing on the other side of the panel.

"Bless me Father for I have sinned."

"Let's dispense with that and get right to it...*They're going to intercept you in Quezon*, so there's been a change in plans.

"You'll find an Avanza on the other side of the Church, with all you need to cross into Luzon—only until Albay—and we will take it from there."

"Thank you, Father."

"Not quite, but I'm from the same Circle as your Dad. I was there at your baptism, I've have watched you grow from a good distance, Richie. There's much to be sanctified with your work, your life, and I've held my tongue when your Mom said to let you find your way: what was that she liked to say... "the best way towards something is away from it." But I have prayed and trust you are where the Lord has intended you to be. I've let Raul and Olivia know you are in good hands. God's hands: we've asked Saint Jose Maria to pray to Our Lady and guide you home, *hijo*. And if—no when —you make it, and finish your duties here, come see me. Our community will have a have a safe, sacred place for you."

"Uhmm, *Tito*, may I know if..." Suddenly, the booth was silent and he could hear footsteps fade away from him.

He stayed in the confessional a minute longer, in a cold sweat. It had been over a half a decade since he actually did the sacrament, he thought, as he tried to close his eyes in prayer. Suddenly, the pang of memory came back: a grade school retreat when the priest, face-to-face, had asked him questions he thought too personal, and started placing his hands on Richie's knee. A long moment, frozen in disgust and fear until enough rage seeped into him to stand up, and run out of the room. He opened his eyes, slapped his own face and shook his head to bury the memory, only to be welcomed with the fear of wondering what would become of the girl as they got closer to Manila. And, if they were blessed enough to make it, what lay in store for him afterwards.

When he emerged from the confessional box to look for her, he panicked when he saw the front row was empty, with the Cathedral doors now opened by the sacristans. He walked frantically across the pews, the saints' statues; and finally, heard barking. Sure enough, Gandalf was there, at the alcove on the other side, growling at a stern elderly, veiled matron, and stood in between her and the little girl who was looking up at the Virgin Mary, both of them smiling.

WITH FATIMAH AND Gandalf now snuggling safely in the back of their new ride, Richie started the engine and found next to his seat, a mint analogue Alcatel phone, a neatly folded map, and a sheaf of papers, one bearing a DSWD stamp paper clipped to a laminated IATF ID. He didn't bother to examine them, crammed them into his backpack compartment, adjusted the stiffer seats, and drove off.

As his thoughts settled from the days past, he cheered himself up with the wry consolation that he was starring in a Wes Anderson film. This time, starring papists of all persuasions, with its own Society of Crossed Keys working behind the scenes as they tried to complete their haphazard journey. This eased the cruel languor from the midday sun as they reached the port and boarded the FastCat to Matnog without any resistance. The *arrastre* mindlessly shuffled through their documents, asking him if he was related to the ferry company's owner, to which he smiled and name-dropped a white lie just to ease their embarkation as the infrared thermometer beeped and they were passively let through .

Just like the first RORO, and not wanting to leave Gandalf on the deck, Richie rolled down the tinted windows ever so slightly, enough for the sea air to waft in, and prying eyes to not bother. He climbed up to the main cabin, keeping his head down mostly, and scoping out the passengers while stocking up on water, and banana crisps, after realizing he had left the *lakatan* stash in the wagon back by the Church.

He then remembered Uncle Leon's last bit of advice as he patted his bald spot with his pyjama sleeves before waving goodbye:

"This administration's henchmen have grown plodding and clumsy, and this gives you enough time. But they will figure things out. You've seen what they can do."

Uncle Leon knew all too well of the pogroms that had begun in his hometown, metastasizing across the archipelago, and into the world's umbrage. "Be prepared to cover your tracks and change course. Pray with moving feet. I trust you will know what to do if it has come to that."

As Richie reclined his seat to reach out to pat Gandalf's head, with hers lain on the hound's tummy, he stroked their foreheads as a way to relax and lull them to sleep on this last ferry ride to the mainland. He reached back to fish out one of the books from his cousin's old stash, and chuckled at the irony when he looked at the cover of one of this childhood staples. Still teary-eyed with fear and comic relief, Richie read the story to the half-sleeping girl: "Fatimah, I present to you an all-time classic, *Digong Dilaw*..."

RICHIE WAS JOLTED from another dream. This time, he found himself on one of those empty ships, wearing a soiled infantry uniform, almost as if he were right in that scene in Dunkirk, with the invisible enemy forces closing in, one sniper shot clanging on the rusted hull, aerial bombs detonating one at a time amid the squadron's descent, the sirens blaring as the faceless bombers dived in to release its wrath on to him and his helpless companions. He looked around, all of them young and old, looking like mere civilians forced into ill-fitting, fetid uniforms; now at the shoreline, making their way to the boats that one by one were being picked off and gunned down by the invaders, until the larger explosions started coming nearer and nearer.

AS HE AWOKE, HE SAW The girl, her head now laying on his outstretched arm, switching places with his snoring dog. He fixed his gaze on her face, and wondered what it would be like to be a new father; having someone of his own flesh and blood come into the world, or taking someone like her as his own. How precious and delicate and urgent it would be to care for a child, to shield her from the growing ugliness that his nation had become with its leaders. How, if he survived this misadventure, he would have to find real work: a career to put food on the table and a proper roof on their heads. He shook his head when the likelihood of him messing up his relationship would likely end up with him raising her alone.

He remembered and reimagined his senior year, filling up the application forms for JVP at the emptied college cafeteria benches. He bragged then to his friends—all set or schlepping through Zoom interviews to break into the corporate world; or their hare-brained start-ups and 'social enterprises'– that he would never 'sell soap' like his older siblings, nor work as a cog in a capitalist machine, to the secret delight of his parents. Richie even thought, more than once, of giving the Novitiate a go. He admired his Jesuit professors, and wanted the same respect and gravitas. But he buckled at the cost of giving up his comfort, his relationships, and the fear of a violent death like his namesake endured a decade before in Cambodia.

He sighed, not just with that fading choice, but also in thinking how stark a re-entry it would be after JVP to go back into the real world, with its post-pandemic constraints, let alone his girlfriend's standard of living and pathway. She, too, was on a gap year: but one spent in a fashion house in Paris. And it was she who asked to take a non-exclusive break so they could scratch their itches, let the chips fall where they may, 'til they returned to figure things out.

Next to that ambivalence and weary affection, his loyalty to and fierce protection of the little girl were a wake-up call. With all the confusion, it was the only thing that made perfect sense. Shaking his head once more, he opened his eyes and saw her looking at him as she placed her tiny, brown hand on his forearm. A thought came to mind from his Netflix withdrawal symptoms, and he snickered as he began fancying himself as a post-millennial Mandalorian with a cryptic Yoda-esque creature whose survival held his future.

He tried to talk to the little girl in her native tongue, to coax a response, even after all the previous attempts during the first hundred kilometres of the trip failed.

For the first time since they had started the trip, when his eyes had been focused on the road and their narrowing surroundings, he looked into her eyes as the sea cradled them all in the moulting sun.

"I will take care of you; I am your family. I will bring you to your new home."

And with his best efforts, trying to muster all he remembered from his language training:

"Panalipdan ka ako ug dili ka nako biyaan."

Richie started tearing up as he realized he had never felt anything as pure and liberating, and at that moment, Fatimah embraced him just as the horn from the ferry signalled their approach to Luzon. The last time he had felt this way was when he had read Tolkien in high school. As he dried his eyes, he allowed himself a bit of a smile. He started fancying himself a Ranger escorting and protecting a little creature who bore the burden of devastating power, this time the truth of memory that lay locked in the chamber of her frightened heart.

RICHIE BREATHED A sigh of relief at the port checkpoint, when the junior officer clearly famished and listless with the weight of his uniform and added PPE, stared blankly at their newly minted IDs and inoculation cards. Even Gandalf smiled back and then sulked back, sensing another long drive. *They haven't caught on yet,* he thought to himself, but shook his head once more to clear the dizziness from the ferry ride, and to stop himself from falling into a false sense of comfort.

As he shifted into second gear, he heard a loud beep, his first message on the Alcatelw analogue:

Unknown: *"Follow the roadmap and drive all the way to Legazpi, and come to Small Talk Café no later than 9pm. Stay awake, and aware—no stopovers, and do not call anyone else. God Bless."*

Me: *"Noted Tito, will do. AMDG+"*

Unknown: *"Quit that SJ mumbo jumbo....Godspeed."*

He estimated the Sorsogon to Albay drive to be about over two hours, and just enough time to make it. They had enough daylight to cross the main highway and into the border.

He turned the stereo on to stay awake, while feeling connected to the world. After switching through numerous stations, he settled on one with a 70s medley and its slothful DJ. He cheered up when he heard Boz Scaggs and Steely Dan, then a back-to-back of Kalapana and Kenny Rankin, almost as if the DJ played them in alphabetical order, and just like his father's CD and record collection. He imagined a time growing up when that music filled the airwaves, without the now commonplace announcements of drug deaths, Beijing's latest encroachment, and how cases were popping back up despite the latest wave of vaccines from the Mainland. and how innocent the times were then.

At about 6 p.m., with the sun setting, the next radio host opened the set with the news section, and the next few minutes unnerved him with the headlines and developments. He could make out some of the words in Bicolano, enough to know they were talking about his little girl, that she was missing, the lone possible witness to the latest murder in the name of the never-ending War on Drugs. The radio anchor stressed authorities were launching a major search across checkpoints, and that she might have been kidnapped by sinister leftist forces out to destabilize the government.

He switched off the radio, fearing he would hear his name announced as an accomplice. *How could they pinpoint these things? I'd been careful enough. Uncle Leon would never turn me in even with his ties to his old friend;* he thought to himself as he noticed and traced Mount Mayon's sinewy presence in the darkness, almost like Mordor and its all but buried, seething anger.

With the palpable silence in the car, he heard one of their tummies growl as they made their way into Legazpi. He finally found the Café after asking the tricycle drivers on the main avenue, and at the corner of the old Evangelical church, he parked the car at the Café.

Finding the place half-empty, they easily found a table a healthy distance away from any prying diners. With the cash his Supernumerary guardian left him, he made sure to order the *pinangat*, and Bicol Express served with pasta (no pork since he moved to Mindanao), and their new special, sizzling *bulalo*, reminding the waiter to save the hollowed bone as a reward for Gandalf, waiting in the Avanza behind a half-rolled window. Just as he was about to pour the girl a glass of citrus cooler, he felt a firm tap on his other arm.

"May I join you?"

Richie shuddered and almost didn't want to look up.

The burly, aging man in jeans and a leather jacket towered over them. He made his way across to the other side of the table and sat next to Fatimah, smiling as she chewed on the *gabi* leaves and shrimp bits Richie mixed in with her rice to dilute the spiciness of the *laing*.

Petrified and comforted at the same time, he couldn't place how familiar his eyes looked even with the leather mask concealing the rest of the man's weathered face. When a stranger at the other table came over and picked up his hand to kiss it, he slumped back in his chair in relief.

"Your Eminence!"

He couldn't contain himself and almost chuckled as the little girl picked up the gesture and also took the old man's hand and put his knuckles on her forehead as his other hand removes his protection.

"You made it, my friend. And in good time. You two are the most sought-after citizens these days, my friends tell me," the clergyman almost snickered.

He looked at the girl and rubbed her button nose with his acorn of a thumb, and she let out a giggle.

"But Archbishop, why here? This is so public and dangerous given the circumstances?" Richie said, almost in half-whisper while looking around the room at the noisy diners.

He suddenly felt a fever coming on and lost his appetite for food and pleasantries.

"Sometimes, my son, you have to learn to hide in plain sight. In fact, we have very little by way of choice because they are looking for her, maybe you, and they're waiting and possibly closing in." His smile was betrayed by the seriousness in his darkened eyes.

"What options do I have, Sir? At the rate we're going, our luck is going to run out. I don't care about me, but..." he looked at Fatimah, who was now looking back at him.

"You have come this far. And there is little left to do but to trust in Providence, and the grace of what happens next," the old man replied.

"Sorry, your Eminence. But this needs concrete action, a plan, and I don't..."

The Archbishop cut him off and smiled.

"What is it your Jesuit mentors tell you? I know them well enough, they run a school near the Archdiocese and are always unashamed to give me a piece of their mind..." He laughed, as he cued the manager to settle the bill. "What's the word... 'Accompaniment', yes, that's the one. 'Finding God in all things,' even the sacred ordinary. Sounds familiar, right? Isn't that what you have just done? And now we will do our share. You will leave in exactly eight minutes by the kitchen door. Your canine friend will join you after this is all over. And you, *hija*," pointing to Fatimah, now sleepy herself, "will come with me."

He smiled again as the little girl gamely took his outstretched hand, and after putting on his mask, walked away only to stop to give his benediction to the manager and the remaining patrons who now recognized their visitor from Naga.

Richie was beside himself, angry and teary-eyed as he stayed put and realized how helpless he was. How his lessons on Levinas and Buber and Kant were all coming back in the face and vulnerability of this Other, this Lumad girl who shared neither his faith nor genes. And yet how he belonged to her. How tomorrow he could lose everything he held on to, including that hope and faith that got him this far. Feverish, he looked down, and started to close his strained eyes. He rubbed them with a used napkin, and right there uttered the mantra he remembered from back in high school:

"Mary, Queen of Heaven, bearer of Christ, please be a Mother to me, now."

As a waitress guided him to the back area through the kitchen door, uniformed men took his elbow in the darkness as a black van screeched to a stop in front of them. The door slid open to reveal Archbishop Fuentebella, now dressed in formal garments, motioning them to come in.

Richie thought to himself as his eyes grew heavy, his forehead burning and his throat sore, how surreal but welcome this all felt. A year ago before submitting his JVP applications, his *barkada* all but mocked him for his sudden piety in the wake of the group's collective debauchery and diatribes on the Church that he dipped into. All he could do was shrug his shoulders, after being unable to defend the endless stream of sexual abuse and other scandals unearthed by and threatening to consume the Pope himself. He shook off the feeling as he looked at the Archbishop, himself falling asleep in front by the driver's side. And, in that unguarded moment, felt a sliver of warmth part of that strange, abiding spirit that all but led him to this temporary grace.

RICHIE WOKE UP in an abandoned van, his clothes damp with the sweat of a fever broken in transit. The Archbishop, his retinue, and the little girl were nowhere to be found. He was at the foot of the darkened river, with a float approaching from the distance—that looked just like the shiny pagoda that carried the Lady of Peñafrancia through the fluvial parade all those years until it stopped in the wake of the virus.

With the absence and all that had gone since, he had almost forgotten that this weekend was about the time of festival of Ina. He shook his head at the thought, that it almost always coincided with the anniversary of the declaration of Martial Law. And then, he came to realize that this very week

49 years ago was where a dictatorship had officially begun, and never really ended.

He saw the light growing, ever so faintly, but flickering stronger as it found form and approached him, as if floating on the river. His eyes traced the liminal space between the water and warm light, and saw the Virgin Mother. She was hovering, right above the ripples, in full regalia, almost golden as the sun. The Lady smiled at him once more, almost as to tell him She has known everything, telling him to let all go. He fell on his knees, lay prostrate and let out all his tears, as he felt a hand softly touch his chin, lifting it so he could see. He was blinded and blanketed by this soft radiance. This peace wrapped in the glowing silence that he wanted to hold on to before he knew to wake up again, and he simply breathed it all and gazed into Her knowing eyes.

HE WAS STARTLED as the van's sliding door creaked open, and Archbishop Fuentebella was there in front of him in full regalia, motioning him to come forward. From afar he saw the *voyadores* approaching, the sinewy, ageless men from his childhood when he had first seen the Lady brought to the waters by these warriors of the faith.

"What are we doing here!?" Richie groaned as he rubbed his eyes once more, upset at his interrupted apparition, and his doubt-ridden fatigue.

"*Ina* wants to do a dry run since she hasn't been back here for some time. And who are we to refuse, my son?" Richie looked down and saw the Archbishop holding the little girl's hand as she waved the other at him, and he could see her gap-toothed smile in the moonlight by the riverbank where they were parked.

"We are all family, Richie, and our love and reach knows no boundaries. It's all been taken care of from here, to our friends in Guam, and soon, her new home, where she will find her voice, tell her story, and through the Holy Spirit, speak truth to power. *Dios mabalos, sakuyang aki.*"

All this time, Richie realized what had been going on. Silent battalions of the faithful, from his parents and their fellow lawyers, to diplomats, to customs agents, submarine captains, and State Department officers under the new White House occupant were working in unison, as if guided by the Virgin's hand, or their love for Her. All he needed to do was bring her as far as he could humanly go. Then he remembered Fr. Noli's first lecture, the day he showed up for orientation, how hope 'whispers to you to take a step to meet the moment when things can turn for the better.'

The dusk-skinned girl looked at him, tried to say something; he couldn't make out the words and as she tried again, he embraced her and helped place her into the bosom of Ina, shrouded in cloudless moonlight. Fatimah curled into foetal pose, and the *voyadores* then nodded and formed a human chain around the Virgin of Peñafrancia. They pushed off with the pagoda as our Lady accompanied her into the estuary at San Miguel Bay and the submerged, waiting vessel that led to the safer shores in the Pacific.

The name 'Fatimah' rolled off his tongue one more time as he walked up the embankment, and back into the waiting darkness.

About the Author

Quintin Jose V. Pastrana, a dedicated entrepreneur, focuses his efforts on propelling the realms of renewable energy, literacy, and investment for start-ups and SMEs. His academic journey boasts degrees in Business, International Relations, and Creative Writing, earned from prestigious institutions such as Georgetown, Cambridge, and Oxford Universities.

As a testament to his passion for the written word, Quintin embarked on a Lannan Poetry Fellowship in Washington, DC. His compelling poetry and prose have graced the pages of esteemed publications like *Esquire Philippines* (2021), *Likhaan* (2020), *Tomas Literary Journal* (2019), *Oxford Writers' House* (2018), Columbia's *The Grief Diaries* (2016), and the *Georgetown Literary Journal* (2006-2007).

His editorial contributions include serving as editor for the National Book award-winning indigenous poetry anthology, *Bamboo Whispers: Poetry of the Mangyan*, published by Bookmark (2017), as well as the non-fiction collection *A Year in Batanes*, published by Firetree Press (2015).

As an accomplished author, Quintin has penned three books, among them his latest masterpiece, *Ambahan: A Love Story*, a collection of poems crafted in indigenous verse form. Notably, *Infieles* marks his debut in the field of prose fiction.

Acknowledgments

The author would like to acknowledge the use of portions from specific authored works in the following stories: excerpts from a speech by Raul S. Roco on February 23, 2003 and from "Prayer" by Pedro Arrupe, SJ ("Campaign Stop"); refrain from the song "Christmas in Our Hearts" by Jose Mari Chan and Rina Cañiza, released in 1990 ("Deep South"); excerpts from the poem "The Wound Dresser" by Walt Whitman, published in 1865 ("Eulogist").

Regarding the sources of many of these stories, "Eulogist" appeared in *Grief Diaries* (2016 edition), New York, New York. "Eventide" and "Mercury Rising" were published in *Tomas Journal* (2019 edition), Manila. "Hejira" was featured in *Esquire Philippines* in 2020. "Valparaiso" appeared in *I, Migrant Journal* in 2021. "Campaign Stop" was included in the Valentine's edition of *Manileño Magazine and Journal* in 2022. "Antidote" and "Woke: A Love Story in Ambahan" have been selected and published in *Life in a Flash,* a compendium of flash fiction from UST Press in 2023.

A debt of gratitude is owed to Dr. Danton Remoto for his assistance in editing and refining this manuscript. The author sincerely appreciates Raena E. Abella for capturing the photo used on his profile and back cover for this book. Her enduring presence and support are gratefully acknowledged. Special thanks are also given to visual artist Poula Sitjar and Ysobel Art Gallery for granting permission to use the artwork titled "All Too Well," which aptly captures the essence of the book and the lives portrayed within it.